CHIMERA

A SCIENCE FICTION NOVELLA

Watch your corners!

LENA M JOHNSON

This story was originally published in "The Forgotten Shifter Files" by NovaLynn Press in 2022. Reprinted with permission.

Edited by Sheena Sampsel

Cover design by GetCovers

First Edition 2024

ISBN 979-8-9916296-0-7 (paperback)

lenamjohnson.com

For all the monsters hidden inside of us.

ONE

COMMANDER GALINA ZANETA stretched her arms and took a deep breath of planetary air. After weeks of being stuck in shuttles, transports, and musty military bases, it was good to be outside. It was a shame she had to stay in human form and miss out on all the nuanced scents floating around on the night breeze.

Behind her, the rest of the squad trudged down the walkway carrying their gear. Sergeants Johan and Chloe walked together, deliberately slamming into each other to knock the other off-balance. Corporal Mische followed silently, her face unreadable but somehow scary enough to ward off every glance in her direction.

Lieutenant Celadon came up to stand beside her. He stood nearly twenty centimeters shorter, just coming up to her shoulders. From where she stood, Galina couldn't see the metal plate covering the entire right half of his skull, and she couldn't see the LEDs blinking rapidly as his thoughts changed. He'd had coarse black hair before the incident. The scars still showed through his now colorless hair, and she felt stabs of guilt every time she saw them.

"All members of the squad are accounted for, and I have verified our flight information," he said, the cadence of his voice as perfectly calibrated as an AI.

"Little late for that, but glad to see you're on it," Galina said.

Celadon only sighed, as he did whenever she tried to get a reaction out of him.

This late at night, the landing pad was almost empty. The tower lights illuminated only three ships. Two of them were cargo ships, which never took passengers, leaving the little white ship in the center as their ride.

Long and sleek, the flattened profile of the ship's nose immediately pegged it as a common model. They were decent ships, not known for being fast. Most freelance pilots preferred them for their easy upkeep, their universal parts, and low cost. The Coalition particularly endorsed the latter.

An older man with pale skin and gray hair stood at the top of the ship's ramp, wearing the plain tan uniform of a pilot. He didn't look up from his transpari-pad as Galina approached. "You here for the Serena flight?" he asked.

"Commander Galina Zaneta. I'm here with the 4th Enhanced Squad. You're telling me this tiny thing is our ride?"

The man glanced up when she said "enhanced," showing the familiar sequence of surprise, fear, and then distrust.

"Yes, this is the *Sonora*. I'm Captain Jasper." Looking past her at her squad, Jasper pursed his lips. "Are you going to behave yourselves?"

Galina laughed loudly, then gave him her sharpest look. "We're the best shifters in the universe."

"Your kind have a reputation for wanton destruction. I don't want any problems on our trip."

"We're not the problem." She slapped him heartily on the shoulder. "Besides, if we have any trouble on the way to Serena, you'll be glad to have us."

"I doubt that," Captain Jasper muttered and deactivated his pad. "But the Coalition already sent payment; otherwise, I'd refuse you passage." Galina narrowed her eyes, but he turned away and activated the hatch to the *Sonora*. "Just get on board. My last passenger will be here momentarily, and we'll be taking off at 2300 hours, as promised."

"Fine," Galina said. "Squad, load up!"

Just then, Chloe knocked Johan completely off the boarding ramp, and he landed with a grunt, still holding his gear bag. Galina rolled her eyes.

Stepping to the edge of the ramp, Celadon looked down at Johan. "Please do not damage the cartridges. We will need those later."

"I know, I know." Johan pulled himself to his feet. "Can't we have a little fun before you stuff us into a shuttle?"

Celadon sighed patiently, one of the few emotions he could express. "Back on the ramp, please, Sergeant."

"Ugh. Yes, sir."

Galina inhaled her last lungful of natural air before stepping onto the shuttle's ramp. While she wasn't looking forward to three days of space travel, her squad had earned their vacation.

Stepping into the passenger cabin, Galina automatically scanned the room. Fourteen seats, five of them already taken. Four pairs of seats lined the far wall, each with a window. Everything was a combination of faded beige and stained gray. Galina wrinkled her nose, glad her human nose couldn't detect anything. On her right, another four pairs lined a windowless bulkhead shared by the ship's passageways that led to the engine room. She noticed three entrances, one with a security panel. That would be the cockpit.

As the team's uniforms came into view, the curious looks from the passengers changed to furtive glances. A sharp-eyed woman moved to the front of the cabin, leaving the squad to sit in the rear.

"Good evening, everyone," Galina announced loudly while Celadon corralled the sergeants. The passengers turned to look at her. "The 4th Enhanced Squad will be on your flight today, so never fear. If anything happens, we will be here to protect you." Behind her, Johan and Chloe chortled. Galina gave an exaggerated salute. "We serve the people."

She saw their minds racing to find some other way to get to Serena. But it was too late. Her grin widened. "Thank you. That is all."

As she sat down, Johan slapped her shoulder, laughing. "Nice one, boss!"

Captain Jasper gave Galina a flat look that she met unflinchingly. He maintained his gaze for what he probably thought was an intimidating length of time, then turned away. "The last passenger is arriving, so we'll be taking off shortly. Please remain in your seat for the safety vid."

He disappeared through a sliding door that led to the cockpit.

"Our trip will be approximately 78.3 hours," Celadon said as he slid into the seat next to her, manipulating the seatbelt straps with thin, brown fingers. "There are no expected delays between Webba and Serena."

"Good to know," Galina muttered.

The cabin door opened, and the last passenger walked through.

A young woman surveyed the room with sharp brown eyes. Her long black hair hung loose over her expensive-looking cream business suit. She caught sight of Galina and as her eye traveled up to Galina's uniform, she frowned.

"Captain," the young woman called.

Jasper peered out from the cockpit. "Ah, you must be Representative Sandoval. Excellent. You're the last one. If you'll have a seat, we'll take off. Oh, and Mr. Kai, I'll send you your receipt in a moment."

A man with long black hair and a black business suit in the front row nodded.

"Why is there a shifter squad here?" Sandoval asked, looking pointedly at Galina.

"The Coalition made the arrangements," Jasper said, then sighed. "There's nothing I can do. I've already given them a warning."

Galina gave her a wide grin. "We're not on duty. You leave us alone, and we'll leave you alone."

Sandoval snorted. "If that were true, then the shifters wouldn't be responsible for so many deaths."

Meeting the sharp brown gaze with her own, Galina said, "If the politicians would learn to talk to people so the military doesn't have to step in, we'd all be grateful."

"We're not the ones who go into every situation with guns firing and turning into animals that destroy everything in their path."

Heat rose in Galina's chest. "You tried to deal with threats with conventional methods," she spat. "Look where that got you."

"I promise you." Sandoval pointed a hard, steady finger. "We will dissolve the shifter corps and stop all the atrocities that the current administration is too scared to prevent."

"You fucking idiot." Galina rose to her full, almost 2-meter height. "After all the wars, rebellions, and conflicts we've stopped in the past ten years, you cannot look me in the eye and say that shifters have done absolutely nothing to protect the Coalition."

Sandoval looked up into Galina's harsh amber eyes and quailed briefly before she regained control. "*You* look *me* in the eye," she said, "and tell me that Diagmar was worth it."

The cabin went deathly silent. Suddenly, Galina wasn't in control anymore.

So, she did the only thing she knew how to do. She raised her fist.

An icy hand closed over hers, the fingers inhumanly strong.

Celadon fixed her with his hazel eye and his blinking yellow one. "Commander, may I suggest we take our seats so the captain can take off?"

Glaring, Galina lowered her arm. "Fine. Let's just get this over with."

Sandoval gave her a scathing glare before stowing her bag and taking her seat. The passengers whispered among themselves, and Galina didn't like how they were all leaning in to talk to Sandoval.

Damn politicians.

Jasper disappeared into the cockpit, and a moment later, the intercom buzzed. "I have clearance to take off. Please remain seated and buckled in until I give the all-clear. Once we're in space, you'll be able to walk around the ship until we reach Serena. A safety vid will play momentarily. I don't care if you watch it or not; it's here to cover my ass. Just don't kill each other, and don't hurt the ship, and we'll all make it to our destination in one piece."

The buzzing stopped, and a tiny projected screen appeared in front of every passenger. Seeing the screen sent a jolt of anxiety through Galina's body. She waved her hand to mute the vid and turned to Celadon.

"Shit, I forgot to send our last report."

"I already sent it, Commander."

"Really?"

"You never seem to remember to send them on time, so I have been completing them."

"Are you sure?" She frowned. "I'm pretty sure I did it last month."

He tilted his chin up slightly. "You did not."

"Wait, was that pride?"

"No, it was not."

"Pretty sure that was pride."

"Shut up!" Sandoval hissed. "Even shifters should know not to talk during a safety vid."

Sighing, Galina said, "They're the same on every ship."

"No, they're not. Not every ship has the same layout; the extinguishers are in different places, the escape pods are never the same..."

"Oh my fucking god." All the eyes in the ship turned towards Galina. "No one cares."

Dark splotches of red exploded on Sandoval's olive cheeks. She started unbuckling. "That's it. I'm getting the captain, and I'm getting you thrown off."

Chloe and Johan burst out laughing.

"That won't work," Galina said, smirking. "You heard him. The Coalition already paid for our passage. He's legally bound to take us to Serena."

A wicked grin spread across Sandoval's face, and Galina paused. At least, to her knowledge, there was nothing anyone could do once the contract was signed. A politician would probably know if there was. And she'd be damned if this stuck-up child would be the one to point it out.

She was just unbuckling herself when Jasper's voice crackled through the intercom again.

"We just got clearance, so I'll be lifting off in about thirty seconds. Please remain strapped in until we clear atmo, and then you can walk around."

Slowly and reluctantly, Galina and Sandoval both re-buckled, glaring at each other, as the ship's engine started rumbling to prepare for lift-off.

Vibrations reverberated throughout the ship, up through the seats, tickling Galina's nose. She wrinkled her face, trying to make it stop, but the vibrations continued, driving deep into her bones. Her fingers gripped the armrest until the thin metal started to give. She relaxed her hold, only to tighten it again a second later.

"Remember to breathe," Celadon whispered.

Forcing her lungs to take a deep breath, she nodded to indicate she'd heard. "I hate space travel," she muttered through clenched teeth.

"Only a few minutes more."

"Damn you and your emotionless brain."

Something pushed her deeper into the seat, and Galina yelped, swallowing her stomach back down her throat. Everything was fine. It was only the next engine phase kicking in.

Celadon's fingers found hers, and she snatched them, gripping them as hard as she could. Joints popped, but he made no sound and didn't pull his hand back.

Pressure kept building and building, pushing her deeper into the lumpy seat, squeezing the air out of her lungs.

"Breathe," Celadon said, raising his voice over the roar of the ship's engines. Out of the thick window, the ground fell away, and the lights of the city faded below the clouds. The humming of the engine changed as they passed through the artificial dome, then settled back to its bone-jarring shaking.

Faster and faster, they rose above the planet's surface. The toxic clouds of Webba whirled around the dome in streaks of brown and red, flashing in the night with dry lightning. The clouds thickened, darkening until the blackness settled into a brilliant starscape, and the pressure on Galina's chest lifted. Able to breathe again, she sucked in air so fast it made her light-headed as the queasy feeling of weightlessness slammed into her consciousness.

"Congratulations," Celadon said. "You made it into space."

TWO

GALINA IMMEDIATELY REACHED for the vomit bag in the seat pocket and crammed it against her mouth. She made it just as her stomach ejected its contents at light-speed. Keeping it tight around her face, she panted, waiting until the spasms calmed down enough that she could seal the bag without releasing its contents.

Now that they were above the atmosphere, Jasper deactivated the "Please remain seated" sign, and the scream of the engines quieted into a faint hum. The artificial gravity slowly came on, and Galina leaned back in her chair, already exhausted. She'd only been on the ship for fifteen minutes.

As her stomach settled, she opened her eyes and glanced around the cabin. Good. They might not have seen her puking her guts out.

"Did you get it all?" Sandoval smirked.

Galina glowered, but Celadon leaned forward, blocking Sandoval from her view.

"If you are feeling better, perhaps there is some water available," he said.

"Yeah," Galina said. "Sure."

Unbuckling with stiff fingers, she pulled herself to her feet and used the back of the seats to keep her steady as she followed Celadon into the rear of the shuttle.

In what appeared to be the tiniest kitchen in the galaxy, Galina found packets of water in the microfridge built into the wall. Grabbing three, she took a huge gulp, swished her mouth, and spat it out in the little sink, then chugged the rest of the packets.

"It might be wise to save some for the rest of the passengers," Celadon said, taking one. "We can't assume Captain Jasper has adequate supplies."

"Whatever. I need to wash the taste of his take-off out of my mouth, and that's on him."

Looking up, the man Jasper had identified as Kai froze in the doorway, staring at her with wide, black eyes.

"The fuck are you looking at?" she snarled.

Slowly, Kai took one of the water packets and a food bar and practically ran out.

"Way to go, boss," Johan said as he passed the frightened man. "Scare them early."

"Shut up, Johan."

With a mischievous grin, he grabbed several packets before leaving.

Galina shook her head. "Someday, I'm going to slam his head into a wall."

"Ignoring the fact that it is a court-martial offense, it would deprive the corps of another trained and experienced shifter."

His mouth twitched, and Galina shut her mouth against her retort. "We have plenty of trained and experienced shifters."

The lines on his face pulled into a forced smile. "I appreciate the support, but facts are facts. If I can no longer shift, they cannot consider me to be a shifter."

Galina put a hand on his shoulder. "It doesn't mean you're not one of us."

Wordlessly, he placed a hand on hers.

Then his hand fell away, and he slid back into his usual emotionless state. The moment was gone.

Suddenly, the lights went out, and red strips around the ceiling and the floor glowed ominously.

"Please return to your seats," Jasper said through the intercom. "The Coalition just put out a notice that there's a disturbance along our planned route, and they have issued me a new flight plan. It'll only delay us by an extra 20 minutes, but you should probably stay seated."

A rumble of dissatisfaction rolled through the passengers as everyone buckled back into their seats.

Groaning, Galina returned to her seat, hoping there were still barf bags left.

An uneventful hour passed. Jasper hadn't activated any emergency measures, but he still wouldn't let them get up. The passengers whispered among themselves as if talking too loud would somehow invite trouble. The shifter squad didn't give a shit and joked as loudly as ever, despite the glares in their direction.

Just as they passed two and a half hours, the ship jerked violently to the side. Galina squeezed her eyes shut, focusing on keeping her stomach from ejecting its contents again.

"What's going on?" Sandoval demanded.

Jasper didn't answer. Judging from the way the ship jerked around, his hands were plenty full.

Galina's stomach floated into her esophagus, and it became hard to breathe.

"Gravity and air are out. I'm working on it," Jasper said

finally, his voice strained even through the intercom. "Hang on."

Through her agony, Galina heard shouts and yells from the other passengers. The gravity switched on suddenly, throwing them back into their seats as Jasper revved the engine and took a hard right. The straps dug into Galina's neck, and blackness crept into the edge of her vision.

No.

She was a Coalition commander. She'd seen battles that would give her nightmares for the rest of her life. There was no way she was going to die on a shitty transport ship on her way to vacation.

Pushing hard against the urge to pass out, she kept breathing, pulling in as much oxygen as possible. She squeezed her muscles to move the oxygen around her body to stimulate flow and opened her eyes.

Mind focusing, she remembered that all transports carrying passengers were required to have portable oxygen in case of emergencies, but this particular model didn't have any built in above each seat. Their location varied on every ship, and she regretted not paying attention to the safety vid.

Celadon seemed to know her plan. He was already up, ignoring the alarm that sounded as he rose. Galina made a move to follow, but he placed a hand on hers, shaking his head. Pursing her lips, she nodded. Celadon's cyborg systems would keep him alive longer than a normal human, and she wouldn't be able to help without oxygen.

The CO_2 levels had to be rising with so many panicked people in such a tight space. They wouldn't survive for much longer.

Her fingers strayed to the pocket inside her jacket, touching the injector she'd hidden there. She wasn't supposed to have it. She always liked to have one, just in case, though it should be in the bag that Johan carried with all the other ones.

Shifting now wouldn't help anyone, not when she didn't know what was happening.

But she couldn't let everyone die. She had to do something.

Sliding the cylinder out, she grasped it, searching for one more reason not to do it. Nothing came to mind.

Just as she was about to plunge it into her neck, air blew into her face. Gasping, she inhaled the fresh air, gulping in each lungful.

As the suffocating sensation faded, Galina slid the injector back into its pocket, unbuckled, and went looking for Celadon. He was helping a woman with the oxygen mask held against her face.

"The air is back on," Galina said. "Status?"

"I believe the ship has switched to auxiliary power," he replied, tucking the used oxygen tank under his arm with the others he'd found. Galina followed as he went into the kitchenette and started putting tanks back into the gaps left in the cabinet. "It may last the rest of the voyage, but I'm sure Jasper will be concerned."

"Let's check in with him. Mische has some technical experience, and the two of you might be able to help."

"Agreed."

"What do you think you're doing?"

Sandoval stood behind them, eyes narrowed.

Rolling her eyes, Galina signaled for Celadon to continue and, turning to face Sandoval, crossed her arms. "Got a problem?"

"This is not your ship. Do not interfere."

"I'm not interfering. We're offering to help."

Sandoval snorted. "What could a shifter possibly do to help? Blow a hole in the ship's side?"

Galina gave her a flat look. "Your tiny mind may not comprehend that a shifter may have other skills."

"I highly doubt that unless it's how to set up a bomb."

"That is one of them, yes, but sometimes we have to unlock doors to let out trapped victims. Or hack a communication system to call for help." She threw up her hands. "I don't even know why I'm bothering to argue with you. If you want to stop me, good fucking luck."

Sandoval opened her mouth to respond, but Galina swept past before she could speak.

Jasper was already at the cockpit door with Celadon and Mische behind him. His eyes were cast to the ground.

"Folks, I have an announcement."

Everyone looked up, and Jasper took a deep breath. "I'm not sure exactly what happened. The alternate course that the Coalition gave me sent us through the edge of a nebula. It shouldn't have affected anything, but clearly something did. As the shifter lieutenant so astutely noted, we are now running on auxiliary power."

A collective gasp filled the cabin.

"We're okay for now and back on track to Serena. But I have no idea what caused the disturbance or if it'll happen again."

A hand rose from the front row. "Did you call for help?" The woman's voice held a trace of a colonial accent. "I'm a journalist, and I have some contacts that might help."

"Thanks for the offer, Charlotte, but I already did. They didn't give me an ETA for when help might arrive. I was told to continue on my flight plan and check in every fifteen minutes."

Grumbles followed this time. "That's ridiculous," Sandoval said and stood. "Let me talk to them."

Jasper gestured at the cockpit. "Have at it. They told me to keep the lines clear. I don't know if something's going on that's got everyone else busy or if other ships were caught in the same phenomenon. But if you think they'll talk to you, I already set the channel. I'm going into the back to see about repairs. If anyone has any relevant experience, I could use a second set of eyes."

"We'll go," Galina said. "Our corporal trained as an engineer before she became a shifter, and my lieutenant has several years of experience with field repairs. You don't need to do anything. We'll take care of it."

Sandoval crossed her arms. "Unacceptable. You'll be outnumbered, Captain. A civilian should go with you. Just to be sure," she added, throwing a hard look at Galina.

"What is your goddamn—" Galina started to say, but the brown-haired man in the third row stood up hesitantly.

"I'll go. I may not be a ship's mechanic, but I am a construction manager. I've done many field repairs in my day."

Jasper nodded. "All right, Asher, you can come. And I'll take the two shifters." Without looking at Sandoval, he added, "I don't want to piss off the Coalition. Everyone else, sit tight. There's refreshments in the kitchen, but I'd prefer if you'd stay in your seats."

Galina made a move to fall in with Celadon, but he gave her a quick tilt of his chin. She nodded. As much as she hated to admit it, there wasn't much she could do to help, anyway.

Falling back into her seat with a grunt, she listened to Johan and Chloe jabber at each other. The two acted like immature children, and she hated babysitting. Tuning them out, she tried to sit still, flipping through the muted vid set for something to keep her mind busy.

But what if there was a threat, something that had affected air and gravity? No, she better check on them.

Turning, Galina found herself face-to-face with Sandoval standing in her way.

"Not you," she said.

"Seriously?" Galina made to shove her aside, but Sandoval slapped her hand away.

"Don't touch me."

Galina looked down at her. "Then get out of my way."

"I finally figured out how I know your name." She narrowed her eyes. "You're the reason Embracia doesn't exist anymore."

A chill ran down Galina's back and settled in her stomach. "That wasn't me."

"How could you let all those people die? I thought shifters were just apathetic, but you... you went out of your way to hurt people."

Galina's jaw worked as she considered what to say. She could tell her the truth—that they ordered her to, that otherwise, the entire planet would have been lost. The journalist would eat it up, maybe even corroborate it. But what was the point? She didn't have to put up with this.

"Get out of my way," Galina repeated.

"No. I'm not letting you near anything that can put our lives in danger."

Galina laughed. "You really think you can stop me?"

Sandoval shifted uncomfortably. "There are witnesses."

Galina grinned, showing her teeth. "And what are a few more soft, squishy humans to a shifter?"

Her eyes widened, but she didn't move. "You wouldn't dare."

Galina took a step forward. Sandoval backed up until she bumped into a seat. Leaning in with her lips at Sandoval's ear, she whispered, "Are you sure?"

The blood drained from Sandoval's face, and she opened her mouth to protest. At that moment, Jasper entered from the maintenance hatch with Celadon, Mische, and Asher behind him.

None of them looked happy.

"What's wrong, Captain?" Sandoval asked.

Jasper pursed his lips.

"Something punctured the main power generator," Asher said. "Some kind of micrometeorite or something. The ship's automated systems plugged the entrance hole but only partially plugged the hole in the generator. We checked it over, and we think we'll be okay if nothing else happens."

Everyone's eyes flickered to Jasper, and he nodded. "He's right. It could be worse, but I don't want to lie to you and say things are fine. Is the Coalition sending help?"

Sandoval turned a bright red. "I didn't have a chance yet. This shifter was giving me problems."

"Don't want to mention that you started it by getting in my way?" Galina asked.

The politician's face somehow reddened even more. "If you hadn't…"

"There's something else," Jasper said. He glanced at Asher and Celadon. "We didn't find an exit hole, and there's sort of residue by the power system."

"A residue?" Galina frowned. "Celadon, can you confirm?"

"I do not have the equipment to test it, Commander, but it is a thick, glue-like texture, clear and sticky."

Galina's blood froze.

"I don't understand," Sandoval said. "What causes that kind of residue?"

"It could be some kind of space debris, a leak from the power generator—"

"Unlikely," Asher interrupted with an apologetic smile.

Celadon bowed his head in Asher's direction. "Which is unlikely."

"Okay," Sandoval said. "What else?"

Celadon glanced at Galina. After a moment, she nodded.

"The alternate hypothesis," Celadon continued, "is that it results from a shifter changing forms. It is similar to the biomatter that is shed after shapeshifting."

"I fucking knew it," Sandoval spat. She spun. "Captain, I demand that you lock up all the shifters until we reach Serena."

"Hold up, hold up." Jasper moved to stand in front of her with his hands up. "I know how it looks, and it may be the shifters are involved somehow. But I'm not a prison barge. I can't lock up anyone. And if the shifters did something, how could they have done it? They were here the whole time."

"That one got up while the 'remain seated' sign was still on," Kai, the guy in the business suit, said as he pointed at Chloe.

"I had to pee!"

"Can anyone corroborate that?" Jasper asked.

Chloe rolled her eyes. "Johan saw me go."

"Anyone else?"

"I doubt it. I didn't realize I needed a fucking escort."

"Maybe that's something to consider because now we have a crippled ship and shifter residue," Sandoval said.

Chloe threw up her hands. "I'm definitely not the only one who got up. You're being paranoid."

"Those two were in the kitchen after we took off." Kai then pointed at Galina and Celadon. "They were there before I went in to get some water."

Galina glared at him, and he immediately averted his gaze. "Captain," she said, turning, "we wouldn't jeopardize a ship we were on. Why would we?"

"Who knows how your kind think?" Sandoval snapped. "Captain, if you can't lock them up, I suggest we take turns monitoring them. All of them," she added, glaring at Galina. At this rate, it was going to get stuck as her permanent expression.

Jasper sighed. "Yeah, I suppose you're right. At least until we get more answers."

Fiery rage threatened to erupt out of her throat, but

Galina forced herself to take a breath. "Fine. In the interest of peace, I'll accept that for now," she said. "But if there is any investigation into this, I want at least one of my people involved. Just so we can rule out any foul play. Bias goes both ways."

"Agreed."

"Captain!"

"Stow it, Sandoval," Jasper snapped. "I understand your concerns, and I hate shifters as much as you, but I refuse to take part in anyone throwing around accusations. Shifter residue might be proof," he added as Sandoval took a breath, "but not enough to clear me from legal action. As the captain, I will only consider irrefutable proof as signs of sabotage. Nothing less. Am I clear?"

Galina nodded sharply. Sandoval hesitated, then nodded.

"Good. Now, I suggest we come up with a plan to figure out what's going on before we kill each other."

THREE

"SO, we're agreed, and no one leaves this room."

Sandoval stood at the front of the cabin with everyone gathered in the seats in front of her. Galina leaned on the back of Johan's seat, resting her head on her hands, her eyes sore from rolling them so many times. With nothing to do but listen to Sandoval bitch and whine, Galina wondered if it was worth punching her way through and going to find out how Jasper was faring. Even taking a spacewalk sounded better than staying here.

"You're overreacting," Galina said for the tenth time. "Are you that stupid that you think we're going to go on a killing spree?"

"I think there's a lot going on here that we don't understand," Sandoval replied. "Perhaps you are innocent despite evidence to the contrary. But we need to know for sure, and it's too risky if we choose wrong."

"Why would we want to destroy the civilian transport that we're on? It makes no sense!"

"We may not know the true reason, but I will do everything in my power to ensure that if anything happens, we'll know if you're involved or not." Sandoval lowered her voice and leaned in. "*Commander.*"

"That's it!" Galina strode forward. Asher and Kai moved between them as Celadon put a firm hand on her shoulder.

"Commander, please," Celadon said. "Have a seat. Sandoval is correct. To avoid any misunderstandings, it is best to do as they ask."

Galina raised an eyebrow. "What if the power goes out again?"

"The captain thinks that's—" Sandoval broke off as the lights flickered. Galina strained her ear to listen for the air system, hoping to hear its steady flow.

"—unlikely," Sandoval finished with a sigh. "Shit."

Jasper opened the cockpit door. "Sorry, everyone. I guess our patch didn't work. Looks like whatever the micrometeorite did, it's worse than I thought. Now, auxiliary power is fluctuating. Asher, could you go check it out again?"

"Yeah, sure."

Galina stepped forward. "Per our agreement, one of ours must go with you."

Jasper frowned. "All right. But only one. The rest of you remain here."

"Agreed. I'll go."

"Absolutely not," Sandoval said. "Captain, you can't trust this one. Send one of the other ones."

"I'm the commander," Galina growled. "I make that decision."

"No. No one is going until you back down or our ship runs out of power."

Galina tried to stare her down. Sandoval was so small, so fragile. Galina could break her in half without even trying. And that smug look on her face would make it so satisfying.

"Commander, may I recommend that Mische accompany

Asher? She is our most trained technician and could help Asher with any repairs."

Galina fixed Celadon with a pointed look. "Yeah, go ahead, Mische."

Asher wrinkled his nose at the tiny, sour-faced girl.

"Mische is smarter than all of us combined. I'd suggest you listen to her," Galina said sharply. "Now get moving."

The naturally terrifying look on Mische's face caused Asher to pale, and he gulped, running his hands along his jacket.

As Asher moved towards the maintenance hatch, Galina pulled Mische aside, glancing around to make sure Sandoval wasn't watching. "Here, take an injector." She slid hers out of her jacket and into Mische's hand.

Her fierce expression didn't change, but Galina sensed her hesitate. "Sir, isn't this against regulations?"

"Commander's prerogative. Consider it a last resort. But something's odd here, and I want you to be ready for anything. I don't want Asher getting hurt and blaming us. Report everything you see and hear."

Mische nodded, and the injector disappeared into her uniform.

Sandoval was whispering to Asher, probably telling him the same thing Galina told Mische. Whatever. They both had a lot at stake.

With silent glances, Mische and Asher entered the maintenance hatch.

"Celadon, with me," Galina said.

He followed her to the back row of seats. "Yes, Commander?"

"Never disobey my orders in front of civilians again," she whispered. "I will not be questioned like that in public."

"I understand."

She sighed. "I wish I could tell. I think you do, but I can't read you anymore. I didn't think the implants would change anything, but you're not yourself. You're becoming a stranger. We need to be a team, Celadon. Our survival depends on it."

Nothing moved on his face. He simply stood there, his face a half-metal mask with one artificial eye and one organic staring straight ahead. Her friend had once been the cockiest and most talented shifter she'd ever met. They'd been close colleagues for years, and she'd been proud to promote him as her lieutenant.

Now his fire had gone out, replaced by icy logic. In the field, in the middle of battle, nothing trumped a gut feeling. Her gut told her that something was going on, and if she'd been able to go with Asher, maybe she could have figured it out. But Celadon and Sandoval had outmaneuvered her. Not exactly the best commander after all. Maybe her superiors were right.

Breaking off her glare, Galina walked back to the kitchen, hoping the search for more supplies would take her mind off what was happening.

The cabinets had come open at some point, their contents spilled all over the floor.

"Dammit." She sighed and started putting everything away.

Sliding the last of the cups in the cabinet, Galina slammed it shut, but it popped back open. Slamming it harder, it looked like it was going to stay, then slowly opened again.

She reached to slam it even harder when she heard footsteps behind her.

It was Sandoval.

"What the fuck do you want?" Galina snapped. "Here to keep an eye on me?"

"Yes," Sandoval said.

"I'm not destroying the kitchen, if that's what you're thinking."

Cocking an eyebrow, Sandoval looked at the cabinet Galina had been slamming.

"It's not my fault. It doesn't latch."

"Perhaps, but there's no reason violence has to be your first impulse."

"I'm a soldier. It comes with the territory."

"No, it doesn't, and it shouldn't."

After a deep, calming breath, Galina gently shut the cabinet, and it clicked shut. Eying it, she frowned when it didn't come open again.

"See? Try being nice once in a while."

"You are the last person who should lecture me about being nice. You've been on my ass the instant you saw me. What's your problem? You're acting like it's personal."

Pursing her lips, Sandoval said, "I was born on Diagmar."

Galina's hand froze on the cabinet handle.

"I wasn't there when the rebellion started. I was on Earth getting my degree like I was supposed to." Sandoval moved to pick up a plate and gently placed it in its cabinet. "My parents were in the capital when the first bomb went off, and they got caught in the chaos when the shifter squad showed up."

What could Galina say? She hadn't been there. In fact, she'd been hundreds of light-years away, sitting in the mess hall when the news came through about the rebellion. Galina hadn't understood it. It wasn't her job, and she had other things to worry about. It was only later that everyone realized what had happened—how they'd given dozens of shifters the wrong orders, then shut down the chaos by force. Thousands of people had died in a matter of minutes. And the Coalition had just pinned it on one poor Colonel who'd just been following orders. Life went back to normal, but the message was clear—rebellion would not be tolerated. A lot of shifters had resigned after that, but the stain never went away. All shifters carried that with them wherever they went.

Galina wanted to say something. It would be a good time to. But she had no words. Didn't even know what she was feeling. She'd spent most of her adult life around soldiers and never talked to anyone else. How was she supposed to connect with this arrogant politician, still so scarred? Celadon would know what to say.

From the main compartment, Galina heard the screech of metal-on-metal.

"They're back already?" she asked, sharing a glance with Sandoval.

"That seems too quick."

Everyone was pushing and yelling. Galina shoved her way through.

Mische stood in the hatchway, her hands covered in blood, frozen in shock.

Galina grabbed her by the shoulders. "What happened? Where's Asher?"

The girl was trembling. Slowly, she looked up, her eyes wide with fear. She turned her head slightly.

Asher lay on the floor behind her, his eyes closed, blood pooling beneath him.

FOUR

"THE SHIFTER MURDERED HIM!" someone shouted, then everyone was yelling again. Galina pulled Mische back, and Johan and Chloe instantly moved between them and the crowd. Celadon stepped forward, hands up in a placating gesture.

Mische followed silently, eyes unfocused, her bloody hands held out in front of her. Galina pulled her to the kitchen while the sergeants guarded the door.

Without a word, Galina grabbed a towelette and began wiping Mische's hands. The towelette turned a rusty red, and Galina grabbed another one. Mische stood completely still, her eyes locked onto some point in the far distance.

"Is she okay?" Johan asked, leaning in from the doorway, his normally joking tone absent.

"She'll be all right," Galina replied, giving Mische's hands a final wipe and pushing aside a lock of blonde hair. "You're okay, Mische. We've got you. You're safe now."

The girl's eyes unfroze and fixed on Galina.

"Mische, what happened?"

Her trembling intensified, and Galina grabbed her hands. They were cold.

"What happened?" Galina whispered again.

Mische's voice was so quiet. "I don't know."

"Did he try to attack you?"

She shook her head. "No, it was... I don't know what it was."

Something in Galina's stomach went cold. "It wasn't him?"

Mische shook her head again. "Something grabbed him. I didn't see. It was dark... I tried..." Her eyes filled with tears, and that's when Galina realized that something horrible had happened. Mische was the least emotional of all of them, even rivaling Celadon. If something could bring her to tears, and she didn't even see anything...

"She's in the kitchen!"

Chloe slipped in as Johan left, locking the door behind her. Sounds of struggles and raised voices pierced through the thin metal. Something slammed against it like someone was trying to break it down. Chloe's face clouded with worry.

"Whatever happens, protect Mische," Galina said, keeping her voice low and steady.

Nodding back, Chloe stepped back and moved into a battle stance. They heard faint beeps from the control panel, and the door slid wide open.

"Stay back!" Chloe warned. Charlotte threw a punch at her, which Chloe dodged easily, ducking under the journalist's arm to punch her in the stomach. The force pushed both of them into the other passengers trying to get in. Galina moved in front of Mische, pushing her behind.

"Hey!"

Everyone froze. Sandoval pushed her way through the crowd. "I know you want justice—and you will get it—but we are not a mob." She stared everyone down, and they fell silent.

Then she turned to Galina. "Commander, please release your shifter to us."

"No."

"We need to question her and find out what happened."

"She didn't do it."

Sandoval gave her a flat look. "I'll need to verify that, and you're holding the only witness."

"You're not going to believe anything she says."

"Why, what is she saying?" she asked innocently, but Galina saw the intent behind it.

"I'm not releasing her to you. We stay together."

The passengers mumbled. The only thing scarier than one shifter was a group of shifters. But Galina didn't care. Whatever killed Asher had tried to kill Mische. Galina was their commander, and she was going to protect them.

"Commander." Celadon pushed his way gently through the crowd. "If I may make a suggestion, perhaps we can convene a council of..."

"No," Galina snapped. "I'm not putting Mische through that."

Celadon blinked his mismatched eyes, and Galina tightened her jaw. He had to see how this was a bad idea. Why the fuck was he taking their side?

"I understand," he said, "but..."

"Lieutenant, arrange for Johan and Chloe to guard the door." She narrowed her eyes. "Clear?"

"We have to investigate," he said in a low voice. "If we don't, they'll suspect us, and we'll have worse than angry passengers on our hands."

Galina's lips pulled into a tight line. She hadn't thought of that. "Fine. Take charge of the investigation. Make sure the passengers won't kill us on sight."

With a curt nod, he turned to leave.

"And Celadon," she added, and he paused, turning slightly

so she could see his pale eye. "If you find anything implicating Mische, tell me first."

He nodded again, slower this time.

With Chloe guarding the doorway, Galina stayed with Mische to clean the blood off of her hands.

"We've been on a lot of missions, haven't we?" Galina asked.

Mische didn't respond.

"When I saw the recommendation from your captain, I knew I had to have you on my team. You shift like you were born for it." She wiped the splatters of blood off Mische's face. "I know we haven't seen a lot of death, and I'm sorry this had to be your first. If you ever want to talk, I'm here for you. We all are."

Mische turned to Galina, her blue eyes dry and unfocused. "Thanks, Commander," she whispered.

After throwing the dirty wipe in the disposal, Galina sat beside her. "Do you think you can tell me what you saw?"

"You'll think I'm crazy."

"Nope. *I'm* crazy. You're fine."

The corner of Mische's mouth twitched. "I wanted to go first, but Asher insisted since he was more familiar with the ship. I watched him carefully in case he'd turn on me."

"Did you find the damaged system?"

"Yeah. Asher found it immediately."

"What did you see?"

Mische took a deep breath. "Like they said. Lots of biomatter. The patched hole in the bulkhead."

"That's it?" Galina's brow furrowed. "That can't be from us."

"I don't know. I didn't get a chance to look at it until—" Mische took a shaky breath—"until a long, white tendril came out of nowhere. When it touched him, it wrapped around his leg. He tried to get it off. He was screaming, and I didn't know what to do. Then it stabbed Asher through the stomach."

An icy chill ran down Galina's back. They only used cephalopod injections on special occasions involving underwater missions. Without water, a shifter only had about twenty minutes before they'd suffocate, so why would anyone choose an octopus on a ship? Besides, they were going on vacation and only had the basic set for emergencies. Had someone brought one of the extra sets?

No. Galina knew her people. They wouldn't sneak on an extra injection. There was no need, and they'd get in huge trouble with the Coalition. If someone had, she'd smack them so hard they'd see their ancestors. And there was no way they would endanger a ship filled with comrades and civilians.

"Did you see anything else?"

Mische paused, thinking. Her icy demeanor was slowly returning. A good sign. "Asher was about to look at the power system. I'd been looking at it right before he... before we were attacked."

"Was there any sign that something else was there?"

"I only caught a glimpse, but I think the power system had a hole in it, too."

Well, that was to be expected. A hole in the bulkhead would mess with gravity and air but not power. Something threatening the power system, though, could jeopardize the ship.

"Can you tell me anything else about the tendril?"

"Just what I said. It was long, thin, and pale." Mische shivered, and Galina felt a twinge of uneasiness herself.

Fuck, *was* it one of them? "Like a cephalopod?"

"A bit, but not like I've seen in training. This was almost transparent and much thinner. And I don't remember seeing suckers."

No shifter cephalopod ever looked like that. What the

fuck was it? Was it some kind of new, experimental injection? In all her years of service, Galina knew that there were developments that went on behind the scenes.

No, she would know about it. This had to be from something else.

"What happens now?" Mische asked, her hesitation leaking through again.

Galina gave her a wide smile. "You're gonna rest here. Get cleaned up, eat, drink. I'm going to have a talk with the rest of the ship. Chloe'll watch over you."

"Sure thing," Chloe said with a grin. "I'll punch any nose that dares poke through that door. Except yours, of course, Commander."

Galina threw Mische a confident grin and said, "Don't you worry. We'll get this figured out."

Mische didn't smile back.

In the passenger area, everyone had gathered around Jasper, who nodded as they murmured. Celadon stood next to him, eyes flickering to whoever was talking.

"We need to send a team in," Galina announced loudly as she approached. "Something killed Asher, and we need to find it before someone else gets hurt."

"Commander, your attempts at protecting your shifter are admirable," Sandoval said with an exaggerated sigh, "but she will face a trial when we reach Serena."

"I'm sorry, I must not have been clear. I said *something* killed Asher."

"Yes, we know," Sandoval replied sweetly.

The passengers went quiet, and a furious fire flared up through Galina's chest. "Are you implying Mische, who is twenty years old and has just completed her first mission as an Enhanced soldier, is a *thing*?"

Sandoval's jaw worked. "Well, I'm not—"

"Because regardless of what you think about us, we are

people. We chose this path because we care about the Coalition and want to be a part of what makes life better for everyone." She narrowed her eyes and drew herself up to her full height. "Because if you are saying that we are less than human, then we are going to have a problem."

Pursing her lips, Sandoval said, "I did not intend to insult."

"Yes, you fucking did."

Her jaw worked again, and her eyes darted away. "Let's focus on the problem at hand, shall we?"

"Yes, the problem is that something killed one of us, and you seem content to just sit back and blame the shifter."

Celadon leaned in. "You have additional evidence that exonerates Corporal Mische?"

Galina realized her fingers were clenched into white-knuckled fists. Closing her eyes for a moment, she gave herself three counts to shove the anger down. She had to remember this was about Mische and her squad's safety. "She saw a thin pale tendril come out of nowhere and stab Asher in the stomach."

"A tendril?" Jasper frowned. "What kind of animal has a tendril?"

"A squid or octopus," Sandoval said. "I wonder where we'd find one of those on a ship full of shifters." She raised an eyebrow.

Galina counted to ten this time.

"Fine," Jasper said. "If you think someone else killed Asher, let's go see if this tendril you insist exists is still there."

"And this time, everyone is going," Sandoval said.

Frowning, Galina nodded. "Agreed. Chloe, see if Mische will come out." Having civilians tagging along might be risky, but as long as they stayed out of the way, maybe she could find out what really happened.

Mische slowly emerged from the kitchen, her eyes uncharacteristically glued to the ground, following the edge of the wall. Beside her, Chloe stayed close.

Mische was still for a moment, then she moved towards the open hatch. As she stepped through, she inhaled sharply, but she couldn't have smelled anything. Jasper's cleaning robots had already removed all the exposed blood, leaving the floor shiny and spotless. A clear dome covered the largest area of blood.

"The authorities said this would keep it sterile enough for them to collect everything when we reached Serena," Jasper said. No one spoke. But as they walked over the dome, everyone glanced down, searching for what they knew to be gone.

Galina leaned towards Celadon. "Where did they put the body?"

"The captain has an ice storage unit he uses for transporting food. The authorities will take custody of the body when we reach Serena so they can begin their analysis."

"Did they say anything about Mische?"

"Not that I'm aware of."

Damn. Jasper had to follow the law and report Asher's death, but depending on what he told the authorities, the squad would face some nasty questions. If Jasper were smart, he'd keep his speculation to himself and give Galina time to prove Mische innocent.

FIVE

THE SHIP'S passageways were narrow, forcing them to walk in single file. With every step that Galina took, she watched for a thin, white tendril to reach out and grab someone. She wasn't the only one, and she caught others looking up and around as Jasper led them to the power system on the other side of the ship.

Here, too, blood covered the floors, splattered along the wall and across the machines. Whatever had killed Asher, it had done so quickly and violently. A clear breach dome covered a large puddle in the middle of the floor. The transparency that was supposed to show the breach now showed the thickening blood from Asher's body.

Streaked in among the blood, thick mucus-like globs of a transparent white material oozed across the floor. Galina couldn't tell which had come first.

"My god," Sandoval hissed. "I don't suppose your bots took any samples."

"They had already started cleaning it up by the time we knew—" Jasper cleared his throat, "—that something happened, but the authorities told me to stop their sequence and treat it as a breach. The dome will keep us from contaminating it until they can analyze it."

"We have a military-grade detection kit," Galina said. "It's meant to identify pathogens and blood content. We could test some of the biomatter. Get a preliminary analysis."

"Your lieutenant already told us about it, and it won't work. It won't be sensitive enough, and the samples would be contaminated."

"Test the blood under the dome..."

"Out of the question." Jasper set his jaw. "No one is to touch anything until the authorities have gone through everything. This isn't exactly by the book, but I won't get between them and the murderer."

Charlotte frowned, her face hardening. "I can't believe how detached you are. This is Asher. We were talking to him just half an hour ago."

"And we need to find out what happened to him," Galina said. "Whatever killed him, rest assured that we'll avenge him."

Sandoval snorted loudly.

"Even if it's one of your own people?" Jasper asked, cocking a white eyebrow.

Galina met his gaze. "It's not one of my people."

"Are you sure?"

"Absolutely."

"Your friend here seems to disagree." Jasper glanced at Celadon, who cocked his head.

Her stomach clenched. "Celadon? Why are you disagreeing?"

"It's simply a matter of evidence," he said, his voice frustratingly calm. "A man was killed, and we are the only known passengers with the ability to kill in such a manner. The material mixed in with the blood could be shifter biomatter. I agree with Captain Jasper that we must wait until the proper authorities can investigate."

"But if Mische's tendril attacks again, someone else will die." Galina fixed him with a level glare. "I will not sit around and let someone get hurt."

For a moment he considered her, then glanced at Jasper. "Captain, I must beg your pardon, but I would like to speak to the commander alone."

Jasper glanced at Sandoval, who nodded. "Fine, but don't go far. Stay where we can see you."

When Galina opened her mouth to protest, Celadon placed a hand on her arm. "Please, commander. A moment."

Letting him lead her away, she followed him a few meters away, deeper into the ship. The passageways were wider here.

"The fuck was that, Celadon?" she hissed when she was sure they were far enough away that no one could eavesdrop. "Are you actually disobeying me in public?"

"Commander, I was not disobeying. You gave no orders. I was simply pointing out the facts to prevent any confusion and to maintain the proper protocol."

"There is no protocol. Find a section, a paragraph, a word in the manual that has anything about a situation like this."

Celadon sighed patiently. "I cannot."

Galina threw up her hands.

"But," he continued, "that only means that we must defer to the authorities. Taking matters into our own hands will only muddy the situation, and valuable data will be lost."

Galina stared at her friend. "You'd put more value in logic than Mische's life?"

"Commander, this is about uncovering the truth, which we are incapable of doing at this time. We must let the authorities study the crime scene and—" He broke off as someone screamed.

"The fuck is it now?" Galina spun on her heel and returned to the group.

Johan peeled off from the group, and Galina didn't like the grim expression on his face.

"Commander, I recommend Lieutenant Celadon handle this." His voice was flat, heavy.

"Handle what?" Galina shoved him aside and pushed through the gathered crowd.

Mische had collapsed against the wall, bent over limply, something dark dripping down her neck onto her lap.

"Are you okay?" Galina asked. "What's wrong?" As she grabbed Mische's hand, her fingers touched something wet.

Blood gushed from the youngest member of Galina's squad, the one who had the most promise, the one that Galina knew would become an incredible squad commander in her own right. Her throat had been cut with one smooth slash, black against her ashen skin.

"Someone get the kit!" Galina yelled, cradling Mische. "Now!"

No one helped her. Everyone just stared.

"It's too late, sir," Chloe whispered.

Pushing her aside, Galina put her hand over Mische's throat, trying to stop the bleeding. In the dim light, it appeared black as it oozed through Galina's fingers.

Mische's blue eyes flickered to Galina, her lips twitching as if trying to speak, but she only gurgled. Her eyes dimmed, and she went limp in Galina's arms. Galina ran a bloody hand through Mische's blond hair, pulling her closer.

She was the commander. She was supposed to protect them. All she had done was turn her back, and now Mische was dead. Angry tears burned her eyes as a cool hand landed on her shoulder.

"I can't remember if she had any family," Galina said quietly as Celadon gently pulled her away, laying Mische on the floor.

"I will take care of her," he said. "I know how you don't like to handle those calls."

He helped her to her feet, and she looked around the group. None of them would meet her eyes. Fury settled into her stomach, and its fire spread through her veins. "Which one of you did it?" she asked quietly.

"Commander?" Johan asked.

"Who thought they were avenging Asher?" Tugging herself out of Celadon's grip, she walked up to Kai. "Was it you? Taking out the evil shifter you think killed your friend?"

His eyes widened, and he shook his head vigorously, backing up until he hit the wall.

"Fucking coward." She looked at Charlotte. "Wanted a better story, one with an ending under your control? You know she was a kid, right?"

Sandoval stepped up. "Commander, this isn't necessary..."

Spinning, Galina threw out a hand and caught Sandoval on the throat, pinning her against the wall. "I bet *you* told them to do it."

"Of course, I didn't," Sandoval said, rasping against Galina's arm across her throat. "Let me go."

"No, of course you didn't. You wouldn't have to. With the right words, you can make them think it was their idea. And you could just sit back and watch."

"Galina!"

The sharp tone of Celadon's voice froze her in place. She'd let her temper get away from her again. But someone knew something. She let go of Sandoval and turned to face him.

His eyes were fixed on her, his jaw working. The lights on his artificial eye flashed faster than normal. As he pulled himself together, the lights slowed to their normal tempo.

"What?" she barked.

"Commander, I must inform you that you are behaving

inappropriately. Our priority must be to uncover the truth, not accuse the passengers."

Galina gritted her teeth. "You were the one saying it could be one of us."

"According to the evidence we have, it could be."

Galina glanced at Johan and Chloe, each of them positioned around Mische's body, glaring down at the rest of the passengers. They were waiting for her to decide. She was losing control of this situation.

Galina slowly exhaled. *One, two, three.* "Johan, accompany whoever wants to go back to the main cabin. Chloe, get some help and move Mische to wherever they put Asher, then join Johan."

"What about everyone else?" Johan asked.

"They can do what they like." Galina straightened her jacket, using the movement to find the comforting weight of the injector. "I'm going hunting."

The collective eyes of the passengers widened.

Galina forced the anger and rage down into a determined focus. Time to be a commander. "I don't know who or what killed Mische, but I'm going to find what started this and end it so we can get back to finding out what really happened."

Celadon stepped forward. "Our time would be better spent investigating the current situation."

"Then investigate it. I'm going to find out whoever or whatever is doing this. If anyone wants to come along, fine."

"I'm not letting you go alone." Sandoval glanced around. "Any of the non-shifters willing to go with her?"

No one answered. Sandoval set her jaw and turned back to Galina. "Guess you're stuck with me, then. If you happen to find anything, we'll want someone to confirm it."

"Love the attitude, hate that it's you," Galina replied. "Try to keep up."

"Should I bring anything?"

"No. I don't want to worry about you shooting me, accidentally or otherwise. The best thing you can do is stay close and watch for the tendrils that Mische saw. Chloe, Johan." The two shifters looked up. "Be careful. Be quick, get your work done, and stay together. Don't give anyone an excuse to kill you, and try not to be on your own. I don't want to lose you, too."

They nodded and moved to guide the passengers back to the cabin.

As she turned, Galina caught Celadon's eye, the yellow one blinking at its normal pace. "What?"

The blinking sped up briefly before slowing down again. "Be careful," he said.

She gave him a half-smile. "Not my style."

"I know, that's what worries me. But please try to think before you act." His organic eyebrow cocked in emphasis.

Pursing her lips, she nodded. Grabbing Sandoval's arm, she dragged her towards the back of the ship.

SIX

A THIN STRIP of white lights down both sides of the passageway provided the only light source. This was likely how Jasper saved money. Running these ships back and forth between distant planets would eat into a profit margin. With luck, this was the only trimming Jasper did to save on costs.

Thick grating along the wall covered the wires, tubes, and power conduits that connected all the ship's systems. Different colored lights flickered and flashed in what Galina hoped was a completely normal way. She knew little about ships, but she knew that the status quo was important. If anything disrupted it, bad things happened. Seeing the fragile nest of wires and lights, she had a greater appreciation for how lucky they'd been. Whatever roamed these passageways could have cut out air permanently.

"It's so dark. Can you see anything?" Sandoval asked as they crept through the narrow passageways.

Galina didn't answer until they were far enough away that they'd be safe from prying eyes. She wasn't keen on anyone seeing her pull out the syringe, but it couldn't be helped.

"Is that..."

"Yep." Galina took a deep breath, held the syringe to her neck, and pressed the activator with a brush of her finger, immediately letting go.

Immediately, the rush of chemicals exploded through her body, the power reaching from the tips of her toes to the ends of her hair. Every cell in her body drank in the tiny injection. She opened her eyes, letting them adjust to the dim light.

Sandoval glowed with a bright red and white heat set against the sporadic signatures of the ship's generators scattered behind the wall grating. Looking back, Galina saw the dim outline of their footprints fading as the heat dissipated. They were alone. That might be a good thing if it were true.

"Aren't you restricted from doing that unless on a mission?"

"Yes, and you're welcome to remind me of that when we find out what's been killing our people."

Sandoval snorted. "Even now, when we're alone, you won't admit it was one of you?"

Galina turned around slowly, and Sandoval gasped. Her eyes, she knew, were now slitted, large, and reptilian. The skin around her eyes was dry, moving stiffly as if covered in scales.

"I know my people, and as much shit as people give us, we still choose to stand between you and whatever threatens the Coalition."

"Even when your body does... that?" Sandoval nodded at Galina's eyes.

"Anything that gives us the upper edge on our enemies."

"And who are your enemies?"

"My enemies are your enemies." Galina turned back towards the empty passageway. "We should get moving before the trail fades."

Scanning the walls, floor, and ceiling, Galina checked every heat source she could find. "Shit," she said finally. "Whatever we're chasing either doesn't put out a heat signature or can hide it."

"What could possibly hide a heat signature?"

"Not a shifter, that's for sure."

"I still don't understand why you think it's a thing we're after and not an intruder. Ships have been known to be boarded."

"Because I know Mische, and nothing can... *could* ever scare her. No, whatever she saw was real. I just wish she'd gotten a better look at whatever it was before she..." Fuck. Galina had seen good shifters die before, but not like this.

"You really did care about her."

"Of course I do. I care about all of my people. Their lives are in my hands, and I've failed one of them. I won't let it happen again."

They reached a junction. Galina flattened along the wall, and Sandoval did the same. Holding a finger up to her lips, Galina listened then frowned. Her human ears just weren't enough.

Pulling out the injector, she changed the dial.

Sandoval looked skeptical. Galina gave her a half-smile in the dim light as she pressed it against her neck again with another light touch on the activator.

Her heat-sensitive vision immediately vanished. The same wave of power rushed over her, and suddenly, she heard the air moving through the filters, the thunderous roar of their breathing, the pounding of their hearts.

"What did—" Galina slapped a hand over Sandoval's mouth. Already, the piercing cacophony echoed through her head, and it took nearly a minute for the pain to subside.

Galina gestured at her ears. Sandoval's eyes widened again. She nodded, and Galina removed her hand. Even the sound of their skin touching was almost too much.

Standing absolutely still, she mentally sorted through the

normal sounds of the ship. She could distantly hear the passengers talking far behind them, hear them walking around. Someone placed a glass down on the counter in the kitchen.

Filtering that out, she turned her head to orient her right ear to best detect sounds from the rear of the ship. Closing her eyes, she clicked her tongue. The sound echoed down the hallway. Mentally picturing the layout, she sensed the turn of the passageway, the power transformers, and the gaps between the grating.

But nothing else.

Galina turned to Sandoval, gesturing for her to follow. Sandoval held up a finger to indicate she wasn't ready. Galina cocked an eyebrow, and Sandoval gestured at her own throat. Ah, she wanted to know if she could speak.

Nodding, Galina held her hand out flat and lowered it, indicating if Sandoval wanted to speak, she'd have to do so quietly.

"What exactly did you do?" Sandoval whispered.

Galina winced at the volume but held back a retort. It wasn't Sandoval's fault. She didn't know how sensitive Galina's hearing was right now.

Pointing at her ears, she mouthed, "Bat."

"Ah," Sandoval mouthed. She gestured at Galina's eyes, which would have reverted to their normal human appearance by now.

"Viper."

Her eyebrows rose, then furrowed.

Impatient, Galina pursed her lips and gestured harshly at the passageway ahead of them. Sandoval nodded and fell in behind Galina as she led the way. Their footsteps were incredibly loud, and occasionally Galina stopped them so she could listen.

Still nothing.

As she raised her foot to take a step forward, a sharp pop pierced Galina's sensitive ears. She froze.

"Did you hear that?" she whispered.

"Hear what?"

Whatever it was, it was gone. But that had not been a normal ship sound. Or any kind of normal sound. The hairs on the back of Galina's neck stood on end. Motioning for Sandoval to follow, Galina approached the end of the hall. Placing each foot carefully to make as little noise as possible, she crept forward.

Then she heard it again, but louder. Turning to warn Sandoval, she noticed a flat, vertical black disc floating in the middle of the passageway behind them.

Galina had never seen anything so black. No light reflected off its surface, if it even had a surface.

Then, a white, pale shape appeared in its center, lengthening into a tendril. It shone wetly, dripping clear congealed biomatter onto the floor. Galina's breath caught in her throat.

"Oh my god," Sandoval breathed. "It's real."

The tendril kept growing longer, at most a couple of centimeters wide. This was what had killed Mische and Asher.

Slowly, it curled and floated in the air, the wetness drying almost instantly the further it went. Its resemblance to an octopus tentacle in the water was uncanny, sending a shiver down Galina's back. She moved in front of Sandoval, keeping her eyes locked on the tip of the tendril, which tapered to an almost invisible point.

Sandoval gripped Galina's arm, her fingers digging into her muscles. A distant part of Galina's mind registered the discomfort, but as the tendril moved towards them, she widened her stance, her fingers moving towards her jacket.

The grip on her arm tightened. "Is that safe?"

"No," Galina replied. "But it's safer than that."

She ran Mische's description through her memory. Quick,

she'd said. Came out of nowhere. If Galina hadn't heard that popping noise, they never would have turned around. It would have snuck up on them. They'd be dead before ever realizing what had happened.

That thing had killed Mische. Sliced right through her.

Rotating the dial with a violent twitch of her finger, Galina selected something quick and deadly.

"Let go," she said sharply, and Sandoval immediately released her grip, stepping back.

As her infrared vision faded, Galina jammed the syringe against her neck and held it longer this time. She didn't wait for the effect to kick in, pushing through the intense wave of nausea and pain as her third injection fought with the previous two. Even though shifters could only take on one characteristic at a time, serum overlap could really fuck with the body. Three was the official limit, though once Galina had done four. It had landed her in the infirmary for a week.

Bones popped and shifted, extended and shortened. Her body contorted, and she bit down on the scream she knew would attract the tendril. Fuck, it wasn't supposed to hurt this much.

The tendril froze, then began moving straight towards them. It was still slow, but the lazy movement was gone, replaced by intent. Galina saw the whiteness of it, the eerie ghost-like transparency. She saw the tip of it better now, thin and needle-like. Whatever it was, it wasn't anything humans had ever seen before.

As her body settled into a simian form, Galina gripped the grating with a longer, agile arm as she got ready.

The tendril shot forward.

Swinging up the grating, Galina threw her arm out, knocking Sandoval backwards, and moved out of the way as the tendril sped towards Sandoval like a missile.

Sandoval screamed, and the tendril followed the sound.

Galina grabbed it with her long-fingered hand, squeezing with a strength beyond that of her human equivalent. Galina expected it to feel soft and delicate, but the rubbery tendril was much stronger, taut, and solid as metal. It fought her grip until all she could do was direct it away from Sandoval, driving it into the grating.

The tip skidded across the metal, leaving deep gouges as the tendril thrashed its way back out.

Before it could reorient on Sandoval, Galina called out, her voice warbling in a taunting howl. The tendril slashed at her incredibly fast, but she leaped to grab the pipes lining the ceiling.

Relentless, the tendril followed her, and she kept swinging, forcing her strained muscles to keep moving, trying to keep just out of reach. The serum burned through her system, and she knew that intense bursts of energy only quickened the process. She only had a few seconds before the agility of the monkey would wear off. She had to end this now.

As she flipped and whirled through the air, her mind ran through every possibility before landing on an idea. But she didn't have much time.

Her simian fingers reached into her baggy jacket, searching for the injector. But she couldn't stay still. The tendril kept slashing out, attracted to the noise she made. If she stopped, the tendril would go for Sandoval, and Galina couldn't let anyone else die, not when she could do something about it.

Ducking to miss a slash, Galina jammed the injector between her enlarged teeth, freeing both her hands.

It followed her and sliced through the air. A sharp stinging sensation tingled across her right hip like someone had cut her with a knife. Then the pain exploded, nearly driving her vision white. Dimly, she felt the injector fall from her teeth. Her fingers lost their grip on the grating, and she fell, landing heavily on her back.

Warm wetness covered most of her left side. Gritting her teeth, she shook her head, dissolving the white pain that fogged her mind. She hadn't even noticed the second slash.

As her vision cleared, the tendril came for her, and she rolled to the side just in time.

"Galina?" Sandoval asked, her pitch rising in panic. "What can I do?"

Fuck.

"I have an idea, but I need my injector." Throwing her injured body up into the air, she grabbed hold of the grating on the ceiling, flattening her body to miss another swing. "Do you see it?"

"Yeah, give me a sec."

Growling, Galina let herself fall, grabbing the tendril in both hands. Landing hard on her shoulder, she gritted her teeth against the pain, holding onto the incredibly strong, wriggling tendril.

"Found it! What do I do?"

"Set it to 46."

"Uh, ok, I don't... oh, never mind, I got it. Okay, 46. Now what?"

The tendril fought her, tugging, thrashing. Its tip just reached her upper arm, slashing through the thick fabric of her uniform jacket. Her blood splattered back and forth, dyeing the tendril a deep red.

Her grip was weakening. Fuck. The simian serum had almost worn off. Her human strength wouldn't be enough to contain it, much less stop it. "Neck!" she shouted, squeezing as hard as she could to keep the tendril from escaping.

Sandoval jammed the injector against her neck, and the cooling sensation once again rolled over her body. Her cells exploded into pain. Sandoval pulled back, but it wasn't enough. Galina grabbed her hand and slammed the injector back to her neck for a longer dose.

Change rippled through her, tearing her apart cell by cell. Every ounce of strength she had went into keeping her grip on the tendril. She had to hold on.

Galina's furry body dissolved into biomatter as her body lengthened. Her human skin appeared briefly underneath the sloughed fur before thickening into scales. Limbs shortened into small, clawed digits, and the tendril slipped out of her grip. She knew she wouldn't be fast enough. But she could make sure it didn't hurt Sandoval.

The tendril pulled back, recoiling for its last strike. Galina's vision shifted into a panoramic view of the hallway, her new eyes piercing through the dim light. Air vibrations through her lengthening snout told her exactly where the tendril was.

Galina sensed Sandoval taking in a breath to scream, so she acted. As her body fully formed into a crocodile, she gave a deep, guttural roar that drowned out Sandoval completely. The tendril shot forward and buried itself in Galina's shoulder, wriggling to pierce through her thick hide. Her roar turned into a bellow of pain, and she clamped her massive jaws down on the tendril.

The most powerful bite force that Galina could think of trapped the tendril. Briefly, she tasted a slight chemical flavor, but it wriggled violently against her tongue. She held on, driving her crushing jaws down.

It was too small, too thin. It dislodged itself from her shoulder and tugged, moving millimeter by millimeter with a strength that didn't match its delicacy. The tip thrashed against the side of her massive head, drawing blood.

Galina's head was spinning, pounding, screaming. She'd taken too many injections too close together, and her body was tearing itself apart.

Still, she held on as the darkness closed in, the vibrations from the tendril's movement so incredibly painful she wanted to scream. Unconsciousness threatened to claim her, and she desperately held on as long as she could. Burning through her serum like this meant she had seconds left. Furious that she couldn't defeat this enemy, she hoped she had at least convinced it she was too much trouble.

Scales sloughed off, dissolving into more biomatter than she had any right to lose. Her own skin burned, raw and tender, and she shuddered in pain. She hung on with her shrinking fangs, fighting for every millisecond she could to keep that tendril from hurting Sandoval.

Finally, Galina reached her limit. She couldn't hold on anymore. The last of the crocodile melted away, and the tendril retreated to the black pool it had emerged from. With the last of Galina's enhanced senses, she heard a pop, and the portal was gone. Nothing remained but the bloody slashes across her body and her biomatter spreading along the passageway.

SEVEN

AS GALINA COLLAPSED, Sandoval caught her. Galina shivered as the pain slowly diminished, replaced by a cold that ate into her human bones. Every shred of energy she'd had was gone. She'd convinced the creature to leave, but she didn't think she'd scared it enough to leave permanently.

"I think you got it," Sandoval said quietly.

"No," Galina rasped through her weak, human throat. "No, it just got away. I may have pissed it off enough that it decided it wasn't worth the effort, or maybe it had somewhere to be. But I didn't kill it."

"The fuck was it?"

"No idea. Help me up."

With Sandoval shoving a shoulder under her arm, Galina tried to stand, but even that was too much. Sandoval ended up carrying her entire weight, leaving Galina weakly moving her feet so they didn't drag.

"What a mess," Sandoval muttered as they trudged through the puddles of melting biomatter. Already, the bots were out, cleaning it up. "Is that normal?"

"Yes and no. Yes, sloughing off of extra biomatter is normal. Those amounts, not so much."

"Why so much?"

Galina didn't answer. The last thing she wanted to do, besides face that thing again, was to have Celadon figure out that she'd overdosed again. And she wasn't particularly excited about the idea of a politician knowing that either.

Together, they made their way to the passenger cabin. Galina could barely walk, but when they reached the doorway, she pushed Sandoval away so she could lean on the walls and face everyone under her own power.

Some passengers were sitting down, chatting among themselves. Two were talking to Jasper and Celadon while Chloe and Johan stood in the back. The instant they saw Galina, they rushed forward, ignoring her protests, and carried her to a chair.

"What the hell happened?" Jasper demanded, stepping forward. "What did you do?"

"There is a creature," Sandoval said. "I saw it. Galina just drove it back by herself. I've never seen anything like it. She must have become four different creatures to fight it."

Celadon's eyes shot towards Galina, and she met them unflinchingly.

"Well?" Kai asked. "Did she kill it?"

"No, but it wasn't for lack of trying." Coming up to where Jasper stood, Sandoval nodded her head. "The corporal was right. Whatever killed her and Asher wasn't a shifter. It was a creature."

Johan jabbed a pain injector against Galina's neck, but she pushed it away before he could activate it. He gave her a confused look. "Commander?"

"That thing might come back, and I want to have a clear head when it does."

"But sir, you're bleeding. A lot. From holes in your body. You're not fighting anyone."

Galina grabbed the front of his uniform and pulled him close. "Then plug the holes."

Johan's face paled. He nodded, and she let go. Digging through Mische's first aid kit, he pulled out a dermal sealer.

Galina turned to the group. "We need to go after it before it comes back."

"We can't possibly have an alien on board," Jasper scoffed. "My scanners are top-notch, and they've only picked up human signatures since we left Webba."

"Then explain this." Galina pointed at the hole in her shoulder. "If you don't believe me, believe Sandoval."

Jasper pursed his lips but didn't speak.

"Look, I know this seems improbable, and we're working with very little information here. But that thing killed two people, one of them a trained soldier." Galina looked around the room. "We have to do something."

"I agree," Celadon said. "Please describe everything you saw, and I will analyze it."

As Johan ran the sealer over Galina's shoulder, she grunted as the open wound burned and stretched. "I appreciate the thought, Lieutenant, but we don't have that kind of time. It comes out of some kind of small black portal, and I think it uses that to teleport."

Jasper barked a laugh. "Ridiculous! Nothing like that exists."

Galina gave him a flat look.

"Captain," Sandoval said calmly. "I saw this thing come out of nowhere, and it looked like some kind of miniature portal or wormhole or something. We only saw a single tendril, so the rest of it is wherever that portal leads. That kind of unpredictability makes it incredibly dangerous. I hate to admit it, but I agree—we need to act now. It almost took out the commander, who is probably the best fighter we have on board."

The corner of Galina's mouth twitched. If she sat and thought about it, she should have been shocked at Sandoval's support, but her mind kept replaying the feeling of the tendril in her mouth, strong, alien, and deadly. She'd need something sharper to pierce its skin and some way to pull it out of its portal completely so she could find a body and perhaps a weakness.

"While the commander heals," Celadon said, "I suggest she and Representative Sandoval describe what they saw in front of all of us. Perhaps we can collectively come up with ideas for dealing with this threat." He turned to Galina and raised his pale eyebrow.

"Fine," she grumbled. Glancing down, she saw the hole in her shoulder was gone, leaving behind a fresh scar. She'd have to be careful. Even with the accelerated healing, new flesh was delicate. At best, it kept her from losing too much blood. At worst, it would open again.

"Commander, walk us through what you saw and experienced," Celadon prompted.

Gritting her teeth, Galina forced herself to keep her voice calm. She described everything but couldn't bring herself to say how many times she had shapeshifted. All the while Celadon's eyes were locked onto her, his cyborg brain recording everything she said and noting all her hesitations, lies, and omissions. His human side would be making judgments, ones she didn't want to hear.

When she finished, she broke her gaze. Silence filled the small cabin until Celadon said, "Thank you, Commander. Representative Sandoval, do you have anything to add?"

"Just that it seemed almost too fast for her to keep up. That thing looked strong and fast." Sandoval looked at Jasper. "I am the last person who would ever trust a shifter, but unless anyone here has any military-grade training or weapons, I think they're the only ones who can even put a dent in it."

Galina grabbed Johan, and he jerked as she tugged him close. "I'm sorry; the blood rushed out of my head for a second. Did she just say something nice about a shifter?"

Rolling her eyes, Sandoval sighed loudly. "Yes. Now tell me how we're going to kill this thing."

"Kill?" Charlotte's face went white. "You can't seriously think anyone can kill that thing, not if it can do what you say it can do."

Murmurs rolled around the passengers.

"While your enthusiasm is encouraging," Celadon said mildly, "I think it would be prudent to conduct tests before we throw everything we have at this creature. We don't even know what it is, much less how to kill it. And it could be motivated by purely animalistic instincts."

"It's not an animal," Sandoval growled. "No animal acts like that."

Celadon inclined his head. "I meant the term as a description only. But I take your meaning. Commander, would you speak with me for a moment? Privately."

Everyone turned to Galina. Her chest ignited in anger and shame. *Here it comes.*

"Fine."

Johan put a hand on her arm to help her up, but she shrugged him off, pulling herself to her feet. She grabbed the seat back to hold herself steady, then nodded at Celadon. "Cockpit."

Jasper raised an eyebrow.

"Trust me, you're gonna want to be on the other side of that door."

Eyes widening, he typed his code into the control panel and stepped aside.

Celadon entered first, waiting patiently for Galina to limp in. As she glanced behind, she caught sight of Sandoval looking right at her. Her expression was full of hate, determination, a deep rage.

The door slid shut, and Galina slumped into one of the two pilot seats.

The cabin was small, just large enough for the two seats and just enough space to reach the consoles behind them. Small digital screens showed the view outside the ship in real-time, the stars moving slowly as the ship limped towards Serena, too far away to be seen at this distance.

"You're going to talk me out of this," she said.

"I am."

"I'm not going to listen to you."

"Perhaps, but I must try."

"Why?"

"Because this isn't what a commander should do."

She kept her voice quiet, restrained. "What did you say?"

"You are not thinking like a commander. You're thinking like a weapon."

"I am a weapon. That's what shifters are."

"No. We don't kill just because we're told to or because we can't help ourselves. Shifters help people by taking care of dangerous threats." He took a slow breath. He knew he was tempting her anger. "Led by commanders who believe in protecting innocents above all."

Galina stared at him. "I'm not going after this creature because I crave bloodshed. Fuck, Celadon. You know me better than that."

"Do I? Ever since they promoted you, you've been acting recklessly. It's rubbing off on the sergeants, and I worry you will make a call that will get someone else killed."

Galina counted to three. "I didn't get Mische killed, and fuck you for suggesting that."

Looking up at her, his face was completely relaxed, as if they were having a normal conversation. "I did not say that."

"But you were thinking it."

"I don't have that kind of control. You know that."

She scoffed. "You're right. You've changed since the accident. I tried not to see it, convincing myself that my friend was still in there. The one by my side when we retook Lexia. The one who dragged me into that seedy bar where we both got robbed and had our asses kicked. The one who stole a bottle of whiskey afterwards and shared it with me as we laughed at our misfortunes."

Celadon stood completely still, his face unmoved, his arms hanging loosely by his sides.

She leaned in closer. "I requested you as my lieutenant because I hoped you would find a new role in my squad. But all you can do is stand back and spout logic and caution. There's a place for both, but not here. Lives are at stake." She pointed at the cabin behind them. "Any second, that thing is going to appear again, and someone is going to get hurt. The longer we stand around and think about it, the less likely we'll be able to do anything about it. Maybe it won't be part of the power system. Maybe it will be the life-support system. Maybe it will be the fuel cells. A shifter would know this. A cyborg wouldn't. You're not one of us, Celadon. Even if your implants won't let you shift anymore, you can't think like us."

"And whose fault is that?"

Her mind went absolutely white. A surge of agony slammed into her, and she was back at that night, leaning over Celadon's bleeding body, seeing the whiteness beneath his bloody scalp, the pink delicate organ underneath. The bloody socket where his eye had been.

"Fuck you," Galina whispered, her voice hoarse and low. "Fuck you, fuck you, *fuck you*."

A tiny muscle in Celadon's cheek twitched. That was it.

Otherwise, there was no hint that he'd just brought up the worst day of her life.

"You need to take a step back," Celadon continued as if their conversation had been about strategy this whole time. "We need more data. This creature is acting unpredictably, and we don't know what it's capable of. Once we determine that, we can develop a plan."

Without a word, Galina turned and left the cockpit. A terrible pain burned in her chest, and she was so angry she couldn't stay any longer, or she'd hurt him. Galina knew her own strength, and even a cyborg wouldn't be able to stand up to her fury. Every cell in her body channeled that rage towards the creature now, the one threatening every single life on that ship. If she didn't do something, it would destroy everything. She was the commander. It was her duty—no one else's.

Outside, everyone sat in their seats, eyes wide. They'd been listening. Cockpits weren't soundproof to shouting.

Galina flicked her eye to Jasper, who stood just outside the door, eyes locked on hers, their intense blue asking a very specific question.

"You can use your cockpit now," she said and limped back to the kitchen. "I didn't leave a mess."

Jasper's lip twitched. That hadn't been what he wanted to know, but she didn't care. Right now, she couldn't think, couldn't focus. All she could see was Celadon's placid face.

And whose fault is that?

Balling her fist, she punched the wall. The impact reverberated through the metal sheeting, and it gave. Something wet dripped down her elbow. She'd torn her new flesh. Fuck.

The shifter kit was with Johan, and Galina didn't feel like talking to him, so she started going through Jasper's kitchen, jamming her finger against the cabinet buttons.

Galina didn't hear Sandoval until she spoke.

"What are you looking for?" The politician leaned against the closed door with her arms crossed, brown eyes watching.

"The fuck do you want?" Galina growled and went back to searching.

"There's no alcohol on this ship."

"That's not what I need." Finding another empty cabinet, she resisted the urge to punch the wall again.

"Whatever your lieutenant said must have upset you."

"Really? What gave you that idea?"

Sandoval pursed her lips and pushed herself off the wall. "Look, I don't particularly care what you talked about. What are you going to do about this creature?"

"Kill it."

"From the kitchen? Commander, we need a soldier. You seem to be the only one with enough skill and power to save us."

Galina's hand froze mid-punch.

"You seem to have a complicated relationship with your lieutenant and your squad. And I'm sorry that the young one didn't make it." The sorrow in Sandoval's voice echoed the pain in her chest. "She had to have been new."

Galina's voice was raspy. "Six months."

"Fuck."

Mische's wide-eyed face, frozen in death, flashed before Galina's eyes. She'd be seeing that image for the rest of her life. The price of caution, of letting others do what she should have done herself in the first place.

The price of command.

Galina sighed in disgust. Jasper's cabinets were filled with nutritious food bars, packaged water, and nothing else. Angrily grabbing one of each, Galina chugged the water, bit off a mouthful of the food bar, and grabbed a towel to dab at the wound she'd reopened.

"Look, I'm having a shit day, and you're not making me

feel better. How about you just fuck off and leave me alone, okay?"

Sandoval had the audacity to seem regretful. Her eyes flickered to the trickle of blood on Galina's shoulder.

"I'm sorry," she whispered.

"Thanks, but sorry never brought back the dead."

The expression on Sandoval's face went melancholy.

"Why are you here?" Galina asked, letting her tone soften.

Sandoval took a deep breath. "I want you to go after the creature."

"I know that, but everyone thinks that's a bad idea."

"What do you think?"

Galina took another bite of the food bar, buying herself time to think. She chewed and swallowed. "I think that I really want to rip it into microscopic pieces."

"Then what are you still doing here?"

"My adviser has recommended that I step back and think like a commander."

Sandoval frowned. Walking into the kitchen, she came towards Galina, who moved to the side warily. But Sandoval just reached into the cabinet and pulled out a water. "A commander looks after her people, doesn't she?"

"Yes," Galina replied carefully. She sensed a verbal trap.

Draining the water bottle, Sandoval wiped her lips with the back of her hand. "We are in danger. Everyone knows that now. But you've faced the creature and lived. You know what we're up against, what it can do." Her voice rose in pitch. "Any second, it could come back and kill someone else. A commander doesn't stop and think, study, imagine. What will you know in an hour that you don't already know? And how could you possibly learn something new about something so different, so unusual?"

Galina stiffened. Her wound throbbed in time with her heartbeat.

"What are you waiting for?"

Fuck. She was right. Even with Celadon's brain, what could he offer her in an hour? They needed more data, and the only way to get that was to interact with the creature again, and that only happened when someone got hurt.

Shoving the rest of the food bar in her mouth, Galina threw the bloody towel into the sink and walked past Sandoval.

"Where are you going?" she asked.

"Keep them together," Galina said. "Don't let them leave the cabin. If they stick together, they'll be able to defend each other if it comes back."

"That didn't answer my question."

"I know." Taking a deep breath, Galina said, "Please take care of them for me." A gentle hand landed on Galina's uninjured shoulder. She didn't turn around, didn't want Sandoval to see her face. "Being a soldier is all I know. It's what I'm best at."

"I know. Good luck. And thank you."

Exiting the kitchen, Galina slid behind the chairs. Everyone was arguing about the best way to deal with the creature. Part of her wanted to throw herself in the middle and tell them how things were going to go. But she was past that. She didn't know how to convince people because words weren't her strong suit. Her language was action, and she had plenty of words to say to the creature.

Underneath one of the seats, she found the bag Johan had been carrying. Quietly undoing the seal, she pulled out a fresh serum cartridge and another injector and slid both into her pocket next to hers.

Resealing the bag and stowing it back where she'd found it, she peered through the gaps in the seat. Everyone's attention was on Johan, who was adamantly arguing for a full-on assault, but Kai and Charlotte were standing a little too close to the hatch. If Galina tried to slip past them, she'd bring attention to herself and get pulled into explaining what she was up to. She didn't have time for that. She'd already decided.

Fuck. Now she needed a distraction.

Sandoval moved to stand in the doorway, and Galina froze. Their eyes met. The corner of Sandoval's mouth twitched, and a strange sense of camaraderie washed over Galina. For a moment, Sandoval's brown eyes were warm and supportive. She knew.

Galina gave her a nod. Sandoval turned towards the group, her face hardening.

"I can't believe we're still arguing about this," she exclaimed then marched to the front of the cabin, pulling Charlotte and Kai by their elbows, turning everyone so they had their backs to Galina before launching into a tirade.

Drawn by her volume and presence, no one was looking when Galina sprinted to the open hatchway. Turning briefly, she looked for Celadon, seeing his calm attention locked onto Sandoval. Maybe she wasn't so bad after all.

Galina ducked into the passageway, letting the darkness swallow her up.

EIGHT

VOICES ECHOED THROUGH THE PASSAGEWAY, but the farther Galina went, the quieter the ship became. Closing hatches quietly behind her, she made her way to the power system where Mische and Asher had first discovered the creature.

Maybe it was the situation, maybe it was the strange connection she'd shared with Sandoval that still felt so wrong. Whatever it was, the air felt thick somehow. Different. The hairs on the back of her neck stood on end. She felt like she was being watched or in the presence of another lifeform.

Was it here? She spun around, anticipating the sensation of a tendril slicing through her flesh.

Popping the cap off the cartridge, Galina slid it into the injector and gave herself a small dose of spider serum. She closed her eyes, adjusting to the sudden flood of sensation as the hairs all over her body began to pick up surrounding vibrations. Her heartbeat pounded in her ears until she could mentally compartmentalize it. Going through the background noises of the ship, she sifted through them: the engine sounds, the water, the air, shifts in the metal, even the distant voices of the passengers. She tugged apart all the threads of noise until she was left with a blank slate. If the creature appeared again, she'd be ready.

Stepping along the passageway, her footsteps created vibrations in her mental web. She slowed, giving her enhanced body a moment between steps to listen. She really needed a way to overlap these animal characteristics, but she'd settle for one that could detect the tendril. For now, a chance at advanced detection would have to do.

It still wasn't enough. She needed more.

Even with time to recover, her body wasn't feeling great. Although she detected the ship well enough, her body was sluggish, her eyesight blurry. Ideally, she'd be doing this after a full night's sleep and no serum running through her veins. Not only was she dealing with an unknown creature, but she was already exhausted, wounded, and pumped full of serum. As far as she knew, they hadn't studied the effects beyond four or five doses. She couldn't remember if they'd said anything about side effects, but she probably hadn't been paying attention at the time.

Forcing an image of Mische to the forefront of her mind as a reminder of why she was doing this, Galina came up to the power system. There was biomatter everywhere, more than last time. A stab of fear shot through her chest. What did that mean? Logically, it meant that the creature spent most of its time around here, which made her nervous. The hole that Asher had found still had a seal around it. A few bots had started cleaning up around the edges.

As she looked at the seal, a thought crossed Galina's mind. Their troubles had started when the ship lost power and air briefly, and Jasper had found the holes. Asher and Mische were killed after that. They hadn't seen the creature until then.

That must have been when it entered the ship. But what

was it? It didn't look like anything Galina had ever seen. Celadon, with his database-like mind, hadn't put a name to it.

The hole was too small for the tendril Galina had seen, much less whatever it was attached to. Had it grown, feeding on the power system? That seemed likely and as good a reason as any to get rid of it. She had no idea how she was going to do that yet.

Her senses quivered, and Galina froze.

Something popped.

A cold shiver ran down her spine.

Dialing the injector with one hand, she slowly brought it up to her neck, pressing it hard. One second, two, then five. The quick flash of pain faded into a dull ache that refused to go away.

She'd have to make this quick.

Her body warped and shrank, pulling her down to the ground with four paws and a sloped back. Bones melted and reformed into an elongated face, excruciatingly quickly. Every shred of self-control went toward keeping herself from screaming.

As the tingling sensation from the spider serum faded, she blinked with new eyes, and a faint scent trickled into her nose. Instinct told her to run, to hunt, to get out of this strange darkness, but her human mind clung to reality, forcing her to focus on the ship's deck beneath her large, dark paws and follow the strange scent not of human or machine.

It smelled cold, unknown. Like how space smelled when coming in through the airlock. But something about it was different, unlike anything in this galaxy—a truly alien smell.

She followed it deep into the ship, using her nose, jaws, and paws to open doors. All the while, the scent grew stronger. Imagining the rubbery texture of the tendril between her jaws sent a shiver of anticipation rippling across her striped body.

There. Something white in the darkness. Her human eyes

probably would have missed it, but her nose told her where to look, and her hyena eyes saw it before it sensed her.

Keeping absolutely still, Galina watched the tendril come down from the ceiling where its portal likely was. It twirled slowly, deceptively delicate.

Once she was sure it wasn't going anywhere, she leaped forward.

Emitting a high-pitched cry, she launched herself at the tendril, clamping her jaws as its cold flesh touched her tongue. Although not as powerful as a crocodile, she had more maneuverability now, and she thrashed, pulling back and forth, releasing her grip to bite down again. As before, the alien flesh refused to give.

Something slashed across her hindquarters, and she screamed, the tendril sliding from her mouth. Hot blood dripped down her leg where a second tendril had whipped out from the same portal.

Pain turned to triumph. She'd made it mad enough to try to stop her. If she could get the rest of the creature out of the portal, she could rip it to shreds and make it pay for what it had done to Mische.

The two tendrils lashed out, and Galina threw herself to the side, using her natural agility to dodge. They were too fast, though, and followed her as she jumped, rolled, and leaped. Fiery incisions exploded in pain across her body.

Fuck. The hyena wasn't fast enough. She'd have to burn through this injection before she could try another.

The creature kept lashing out, forcing Galina to move as fast as she could. Her fur became wet with blood from dozens of small wounds. She had to know where both tendrils were. If she lost track of one, she'd be dead.

Taking a tendril in the shoulder, she screamed, hearing the pitch change slightly. The serum was wearing off.

Snapping her jaws, she caught the end of one tendril and

bit down to keep it from slipping out. Blood filled her mouth as its tip cut through her gums. She heard her own blood dripping to the ground even as she hung on, feeling the incredible power behind the creature as it tried to pull away.

Galina tugged with all her strength, and the tendril stayed locked in her powerful bite. But she slid along the ground towards the portal, unable to counter the creature's strength. The second tendril lashed out at her, and she could only shift slightly to keep it from puncturing vital organs.

Her paws slipped in puddles of her own blood. In a few seconds, she'd start changing back into a human, and she'd be at her weakest. If she timed it right, she could move out of the way and retreat, assuming the creature wasn't able to sense body heat or track blood. At present, that seemed very unlikely. Either that, or she'd make a last stand here and become just another corpse, leaving the creature free to kill the rest of the passengers.

As the last of her strength faded, her body changed back. Her fingers elongated, the bones melting and reforming. Her eyesight dimmed, and her back legs lengthened. The instant her jaws shrank, she let go. Galina threw herself backwards, crawling and stumbling on newly formed human legs to find safety around the corner.

Her lungs gasped for air, the pain of her wounds nearly crushing her into unconsciousness. Forcing her eyes to stay open, she watched for the nightmare to snake around the wall, searching for her dying body.

There. A pale tip, visible even to her unmodified eyes, wrapping around the wall. Whatever it used to hunt, it didn't seem used to hunting an injured animal, or it would have pounced on her.

Her jacket was just past her toes. Slowly, she bent forward, clenching her jaw to bite down on a scream. Fresh blood spurted from her wounds as she reached for the injector.

It sensed her now, the tip creeping right towards her.

The injector slipped from her hands. She gasped for breath, unable to hold it in, tears of rage, pain, and fear mixing with the blood.

Her fingers closed around the injector. Muscle memory twisted the dial, and she jammed it against her throat.

The scream she'd been holding in ripped out of her lungs.

As her body reformed again, the pain changed, no less excruciating but a relief from the sharp wounds covering her. The tendril oriented to her and darted forward.

But she wasn't there.

Spreading her wings, she launched herself up, screeching as she slammed into the ceiling. Hawks weren't suited for narrow passageways, but it was the only thing she could think of. Crushing jaws may not puncture the alien's hide, but perhaps sharp talons could.

She dove, biting at the tendril and grasping at it with her talons. The stiff, rubbery texture gave, and she gave a piercing cry of triumph. Sharp eyesight saw a light blue liquid oozing from where she'd hurt it.

Dodging through the pair of tendrils, Galina looped and flitted, giddy with loss of blood and knowing she'd finally gotten the upper hand.

Something slammed into her head and pinned her to the floor. As quick as she'd been, the creature was faster.

One tendril held her down, the other curling to aim at her. It was going to stab her.

Screeching, she clawed and bit at the tendril holding her, ripping through its flesh. Soon, its thick blood or hemolymph or whatever was all over her body and in her mouth. It tasted foul, a sharp, acrid taste that burned the back of her throat. Still, she fought back as the tendril tried to hold her down while writhing in pain.

The second tendril came down lightning fast, and her

hawk reflexes gave her just enough warning to move her head out of the way. It slashed through the feathers on her head and buried itself in the metal, squealing against the grating. The metal held, and the tendril jerked.

It was stuck.

Knowing she didn't have much time until the tendril was free, she put all her effort into ripping apart the one holding her down. Only a few strands of flesh held the tendril together, and she ripped at it with her beak until it gave way.

It pulled back, thrashing in pain, and Galina threw herself into the air.

She was too weak, and the torn tendril caught her again, slamming her into the wall. Falling to the ground, she couldn't move. Her eyesight was fading, and she knew it wasn't just from the serum wearing off.

She was dying.

Cutting off the tip of the tendril wasn't enough. She'd hurt it, but not enough to convince it to leave. The tendrils had to be attached to a larger body, and if she could get to that, she could kill it.

Mind racing, she tried to think of what she could become that would work. A tiger? Too big and too slow. She'd barely fit in the passageway, and she'd be an easy target.

The tendrils reoriented, the one that still had its razor-sharp tip whipping around, trying to find her. The other tendril was retreating back towards its portal. Would it send out another one?

With the last of her hawk eyesight, she saw a dozen white streaks emanating from the portal.

Her heart stopped, and a heavy weight seemed to pull her to the ground. She barely noticed the pain as her bones once again reformed. This was it. Her human eyes saw death coming for her.

Part of her accepted her fate, knowing her body was too

broken to fend off an attack. She'd never had to fight this hard before, and she'd gone past every safety dosage limit. That alone would kill her, and yet it wasn't enough.

But something burned deep in her stomach.

Rage.

She would not give up. Not now. She'd hurt it badly enough to piss it off. It wasn't impregnable. She could beat it if she could just reach the injector and pick the right animal. This fucking thing would die even if she had to take it down with her.

Rolling to the side, she dodged dozens of tendrils stabbing violently at the ground indiscriminately. It couldn't find her, so it settled for a full blitz.

Some found their mark, slicing along her side, arms, legs, scalp. She dodged as best she could, trying to get to the injector.

It lay in the middle of the passageway, rolling side to side as the force of the tendrils hitting the deck vibrated through the metal. Galina threw herself at it, bringing it to her chest. Moving the dial with her thumb, it clicked.

Fuck. It was broken.

The other injector had been in her jacket pocket, but where was her jacket now?

A tendril sliced across her cheek. To die by a thousand cuts. Just fucking great. Her stupid human eyes couldn't see anything, just the ghost-like whiteness of the tendrils stabbing into everything.

There. Her jacket was behind the wall of tendrils.

How could she get through? Like a tidal wave, the mass of tendrils was getting closer. Galina stared at the wave. She only had a few seconds to find a way through. Was there a gap up by the ceiling? Yes, but she couldn't leap that far, even on a good day. A gap along the side? No, the tendrils were stabbing everything, floor and walls. Her only chance was to go over.

Taking a deep breath, she tried not to wince as the motion stretched her torn body. She shut everything out but her goal. *Breathe in, breathe out.*

As the wave reached her, Galina inhaled and ran forward just as a tendril stabbed where she'd been standing.

Grasping, she caught one and swung back, letting go as momentum threw her forward. The creature was onto her now, and she heard the mass of tentacles change direction, the sound of slicing metal stopping.

They were slicing her again, and she leaped from tendril to tendril, grabbing to keep her balance, knowing that she had to keep moving or she'd be dead.

Then the tendrils were gone, and she fell through the air, landing hard on her hip. Her fragile bones jarred, forcing the air out of her lungs in a silent scream.

One stabbed through her calf, pinning her to the grating.

But she'd landed on something soft. Her jacket! Fingers dug through the fabric to find the other injector.

Another stabbed through her hand. Gasping, she used her other hand to grab the injector, dial it, and hold it against her neck.

Every cell burst, destroying her from the inside out. Something icy and foul stabbed her in the stomach. Was that it? The final blow that took her out right before her body collapsed into a pile of biomatter?

The icy sensation grew, spreading to her fingers, her toes, and her spine. As the pain lessened, she felt herself finally die.

NINE

FIRST, there was darkness. Nothing.

Then, something.

Sensation.

Awakening.

The Being felt that it was alive.

It heard everything, sensed everything.

Outside, the Being sensed a Nothing. Cold, airless, empty. Worthless.

But here, it was warm.

It inhaled experimentally, felt enormous lungs expand, felt the surge of oxygen in its body. Plenty of air, although it sensed that it didn't need it to survive.

Then, it felt the power.

Strength flowed through its body, rushing into every corner, every crevice, every cell. It stretched, sending a pleasant sensation to its mind.

Opening its eyes, it examined its surroundings. It knew it was on a ship, knew that it floated in space. The concept meant little to such a mighty being.

Cold walls, cold floors. Hard, solid. Faint sounds came

from pockets in the walls and farther away. It saw the heat signatures of the pathetic lifeforms on the other side of the ship. Humans. No claws, no teeth to speak of. Worthless.

A sharp sensation pricked at its shoulder. It reached with large, clawed hands and grasped the pale, heatless thread that stuck to its thick skin. Through its touch, the Being sensed the thread was attached to a creature half-hidden in another part of reality.

Incredible rage exploded through the Being's body, the flow of power flooding like a swollen river. After the rage came glee, desire, lust for destruction. This pitiful creature may have picked a fight, but the Being would take great pleasure in smashing it and establishing which of them was dominant.

Plucking the tendril from its shoulder with large but dexterous fingers, the awakened Being pulled. The creature screamed in a pitch only the two of them could hear. Its cry of pain and rage emboldened the Being, and it yanked again, pulling the thin white tendril like a rope.

More tendrils appeared, slashing and stabbing. Roaring with pain and rage, the Being tried to grasp all of them, but there were too many.

It decided to end this quickly before more annoyances would appear. Pulling itself towards the origin of the tendrils, the Being walked forward, taking large, lumbering steps with enormous, mismatched feet.

The passageways were so small. To make room, the Being punched upwards, ripping through the metal grating above so it could stand up straight. All the while, the tendrils slashed out, cutting through thick skin.

It broke through to a larger, warmer room. There was plenty of space here, and the source of the irritating threads came from a black oval floating by the large metal tubes that glowed with intense heat.

A bright light appeared, and the Being growled in annoyance. Dark forms with distinct heat signatures emerged, looking up at the Being. They gave off scents of fear and terror.

"The fuck is that?" one of them exclaimed.

"Nobody said there were two of them!"

"There aren't two of them; this one is different," a calm voice said. "They're fighting."

Their incessant warbling was yet another annoyance, and the Being decided that it was through with dealing with all these troublesome interferences.

It raised a hand to swipe at the tiny creatures, but something forced it to hold back. Every fiber said it had the power and the right to destroy whatever it wanted. But something wanted these tiny creatures to survive.

No, an inner voice seemed to say. *Let them live. Destroy anything else, but make sure they live.*

That was an illogical thought. The Being had the power to decide the fate of any creature, so why should it not wipe out these? They were too small to be a threat, therefore, too small to be worth saving.

Despite its desire for destruction, the Being decided it would leave these creatures alone for now. The bigger annoyance required its attention.

Tendrils flew out now, wrapping themselves around the Being, squeezing, slicing, stabbing. Roaring in rage, the Being threw off the tendrils, grasping them in both hands and ripping. The strands parted, and the creature screamed, louder and in a deeper register.

"Oh my god, it's ripping that thing to shreds!"

"I thought nothing could penetrate its hide!"

"Galina couldn't make a dent in it. I don't know where that thing came from, but whatever it is, it can do what a shifter commander with years of experience couldn't."

Grasping at more and more tendrils, the Being ripped all

of them, shivers of delight rippling through its massive body as the creature screamed, its pitch changing from anger to pain. The Being liked to hear its screams. But it wanted more.

Plowing through a sea of tendrils, the Being lunged forward, aiming for the source of the tentacles. There, in a corner of the room, it saw the flat shape, black and cold. Its extra senses knew it led elsewhere, that it wasn't a shadow and led to the reality from which the creature had originated.

The Being reached into the blackness, only able to reach in to its shoulders before it sensed the uncomfortable tug of reality. It would have to stretch that if it wanted to go in further.

But there was no need. Its searching hand found something larger, something not made of tendrils. It was less impenetrable and gave under the Being's fingers. The creature trembled, and a thrill surged through the Being's muscles, tingling through every cell in its mismatched body.

The Being yanked the form out of the portal with a roar of triumph. Its eyes saw the swirls of color across the entire spectrum, across the true body of this creature. It withered in the physical constraints of this reality, forces that its tough tendrils could handle, but its soft body could not.

Knowing it was in the hands of a far superior being, the creature went into a frenzy, thrashing its tendrils around. The body kept producing tendrils yet didn't lose mass, something the voice in the back of the Being's mind noted with dread. The Being itself didn't care. It ignored the slashing tendrils and grasped the body with two hands, leaving its other hands to grasp the tendrils.

Some lashed out at the tiny creatures. The Being wanted to focus on the creature it was about to destroy, but that same voice in the back of its mind screamed, demanding it protect the tiny things.

The Being scoffed. Why should it care for them? They were meaningless, weak, defenseless. They served no purpose besides some fun later once it had destroyed the tendril creature.

No, the voice insisted. *Save them. Protect them.*

The Being felt strangely torn, and that angered it.

Throwing out one hand, it slammed against one of the tiny creatures. *See how pathetic they were.* Barely worth the joy of wiping them out.

The force of will in the voice grew and grew, and the Being found itself pulling its arm back. What was happening?

Taking advantage of the Being's distraction, the creature gathered all its tendrils together and thrust all of them towards the Being's chest.

Out of instinct, the feathered skin on its chest rippled and became a mollusk shell, the hardest material it could make. The mass of tendrils slammed against its shell with incredible speed. The Being slid back, its claws digging into the metal grating on the floor. Metal squealed and spiraled as the Being kept itself standing.

The tendrils slid off, some slicing through the Being's unprotected areas, but its skin rippled and turned into shell material across its entire body. Nothing made it through, and the creature retracted its tendrils.

Still holding the body in its hands, the Being, enraged at having been so blatantly attacked, roared, the vibrations from its throat causing the surrounding metal to shudder in an echoing cacophony. The tiny lifeforms below screamed, putting their tiny hands over their ears.

Thick blue blood oozed out as the Being slid its claws into the creature. It thrashed, sending out volley upon volley of tendrils, screaming as the Being pulled it apart.

Finally, with a tremendous crack, the creature broke in half, blue blood exploding to cover the entire room.

The Being roared in triumph, holding the two halves up high before throwing them to the ground. Released from its normal reality, the creature's torn and broken body collapsed, melting into a half-biomatter, half-tendril mass. A few of the tendrils twitched in a death spasm before becoming completely still.

Standing over its dead opponent, an incredible rush of power came over the Being. Looking around, it searched for the next opponent it could destroy. But only the tiny creatures staring up at it in horror remained.

Their fear delighted it. Since there wasn't anything else to conquer, it might stomp on these noisy pests.

But the voice again demanded the Being leave them alone. Its eyes drifted and saw the portal still hanging in the air, its deep coldness promising other intruders. Glee filled the Being, but the voice drowned it out. The portal led to another reality full of other terrible creatures that it could destroy, yes, but the Being had to close it.

The urge to fight shifted to the portal. Closing it would be pleasurable, removing the creature's pathway from its reality to here.

The Being sensed uncertainty from the voice, and it smugly lay its hands on the portal. The portal shrank, the Being's clawed hands on its edge, pushing it in on itself. It resisted, the pathway not readily responsive to the Being's mysterious force. When it was too small to hang onto, the Being grasped it in one hand, closed its fingers into a fist, and squeezed.

The Being felt the portal collapse, and the pinhole disappeared. The pathway was closed, so it let go. No black oval hung in the air. It was gone.

Quiet surrounded the Being. Only the fast heartbeats of the tiny lifeforms and the natural workings of the ship registered against the backdrop of the sounds of the universe outside. The calm was welcome for a moment, then the Being began to crave.

It turned its head, drawn to the panicked heartbeats of the tiny creatures. One gasped, another moved to place itself in front of the others.

Cocking its head, the Being perceived every biological sound these creatures made. It sensed their fear, their dread. It heard the blood rushing through their veins, the sound of their muscles tightening. They knew they would die, and that excited it. It bathed in their fear, turning its attention to each of them, absorbing their horror until it needed more.

Pushing through the small crowd, it brushed its fingers up against each of them. It changed its skin into sensitive cells, picking up every electrical charge, detecting the changes in body chemistry as they stifled their screams. Oh, this was delicious.

One creature kept trying to push itself in front of the others as if offering itself. This one seemed less afraid than the others. The Being picked it up, curious how a creature so small could hide its emotions so well.

Its fingers wrapped around the tiny creature, and it gave an experimental squeeze. Emitting a grunt of pain, the creature looked up at the Being.

"Don't do this, Galina. Let it go."

Galina. A wave of recognition rolled over the Being. A familiar word. Scattered memories emerged, but what use were memories to such a magnificent being?

The voice in the back of its mind, however, reacted strongly. Almost too strongly. For a moment, the Being stopped, losing control of its body.

"Galina," the creature said again.

The syllables reverberated through the Being's body. It didn't like that feeling. The voice grew stronger, tugging. The Being's fingers loosened, and it roared in rage. Reforming its tail into a giant stinger, it lashed out, driving its poison-laden tip into the skull of the creature it held.

At last, the creature fell silent. The Being let it fall to the ground, where the other pathetic lifeforms gathered around it. A deep laugh rumbled in the Being's stomach, then halted, the breath caught in its throat.

"*No.*"

The voice now spoke through the Being's own fanged maw.

"*I will not allow this to happen.*"

Incredible pain flashed across its skin, and its cells exploded. Roars of rage rose to screams of pain.

Flesh melted off as enormous slabs of biomatter. Piece after piece sloughed off. The Being felt itself falling apart, felt each cell separating. Nerves so recently formed were no less functional, and it felt everything.

It closed its eyes, wishing for death to end the agony. It ripped its own flesh to end the pain sooner, gouging its own eyes out with claws that ripped down its face, parting the flesh. Its massive body shrank, dropping horns, claws, teeth, and its tail with wet sounds like ripping bones.

As it collapsed, its consciousness shifted, condensing into a tiny form inside—its true body.

TEN

GALINA'S FLESH was cold and raw, and she coughed as biomatter filled her throat. The pain had lessened, but barely. She reached out with a trembling hand. Something brushed by her fingertips, and she latched onto it.

It was a hand.

She tried to pull, but she had no strength. The hand pulled her towards it, and arms wrapped around her shoulders. A comforting scent filled her sensitive olfactory system, bringing back intense memories from years before.

"How bad was it?" she rasped.

"Don't think about it," Celadon said, his voice quiet and by her ear. "It's over now."

She dug her fingers into his shoulder, the touch of his uniform grating against her sensitive skin.

Lowering her voice, she asked, "Did I kill anyone?"

Celadon pulled her closer, his lips on her hair. "No. No, you didn't kill anyone."

A sob broke loose, and she buried her face in his chest. He let her cry, placing a gentle hand on the back of her head and holding her close.

"Can you stand?" he asked gently.

Coughing, she nodded. "I think so."

With his help, she struggled to her feet. The room spun. Only Celadon's arm around her waist kept her from collapsing on the floor.

Fuzzy shapes slowly sharpened into the bloodless faces of the passengers, all staring at her with wide eyes filled with fear. Distrust. Revulsion.

Galina looked away. She couldn't bear to see them stare at her like that. She was used to getting stares for her height and her boisterous personality, but nothing like this. Especially when she knew she deserved it.

Celadon led her to the passenger cabin and helped her into a chair. Her clothes were gone—destroyed by the transformation, she supposed. He brought her a blanket, food, and water, holding her shaking hands in his so she could drink. Coughing, she spat out biomatter and choked when she realized it was tinged blue.

She glanced at the doorway, a faint wave of relief rolling over her when she saw it was closed.

"Johan and Chloe are guarding the other side," Celadon explained, noticing her furtive glances. "They'll keep everyone away."

"For how long?" she rasped. Forcing herself to grasp the cup, she took it from Celadon's hand and brought it to her lips.

He took a careful breath. "What we witnessed will be unbelievable to the Coalition. If you can remember what happened, that will help us deal with the consequences."

Hiding her face in her cup, Galina thought back to the transformation. "It's like a dream. It's blurry, and it doesn't make sense." She remembered the rage, the sense of power. "I don't think I can remember anything important."

Suddenly Celadon grasped her chin and tilted her head.

His thumb ran against her neck, tracing all the angry red marks left from the injector. She went hot.

His eyes locked onto her, and she couldn't tell if he was angry or concerned. "How many, Galina?"

"I had to—"

"How many?"

Slowly, she said, "I don't remember. Maybe seven?"

"Seven?"

"*I had to.*" Galina closed her eyes against a wave of exhaustion. "Nothing else affected that thing."

"They don't forbid multi-doses for fun," Celadon said, a note of something in his voice. Anger? Chastisement?

"It feels about as bad as you'd think." Breathing slowly, she said, "Is the corpse of the tendril creature quarantined?"

"Jasper had his bots enclose it like they did for the first attack." He paused, and Galina opened her eyes. His mouth curved in a half-frown.

"What?" she asked, her blood running cold. "What did you learn?"

His yellow eye pulsed briefly in a specific pattern before returning to its normal non-blinking status. He had just scanned for listeners.

"No one has ever seen a creature like that," he said finally, his voice low. "It's not from this universe."

A chill ran down Galina's spine as she thought back to the black portal and the snatches of memories from when she'd been that terrifying being. "It must be from another reality."

Celadon cocked his head. "Explain."

"I think whatever I became sensed it. Somehow, it knew it had to close that portal."

"If that's true, it must have somehow entered our reality when the captain made that course correction."

"There was that jolt. We just assumed it was a hiccup in the system."

"Apparently not."

She shivered. "So, what happens now?"

"The ship is limping, but we're on course for Serena. A containment team will meet us there. I expect they will subject all of us, especially you, to intense questioning."

"Yeah. Great."

The corner of his mouth twitched. "You saved us, Galina. They won't be able to deny that."

She snorted. "They'll try, but I'm glad no one else got killed. Good thing that one of the side effects of so many doses is to turn into one mashed-up creature." She shivered at the lie.

Cocking his head again, Celadon said, "That's not one of the side effects. Every study has ended in intense pain and permanent damage. Never an overlap."

Something cold settled into her stomach. "Then what the fuck happened?"

"I think it was the creature's blood." Sandoval was suddenly there, kneeling and wiping at the dried biomatter and dark red blood on Galina's arm.

"I thought the sergeants were guarding the door."

Sandoval gave her a weak grin. "I'm a good talker."

"Alien blood seems a highly unlikely culprit," Celadon said.

Sandoval shrugged. "You were covered in that blue stuff. I'm no scientist, but with your wounds, there's no way it couldn't have entered your system. As your android would say, it's the only unknown variable."

"I am not an android."

"Whatever."

Galina looked up at her in a panic. "Are you going to tell the news?"

Sandoval frowned. "Why?"

"Full exposure, no secrets, all that stuff." The pain in her stomach spread. "Please don't tell anyone."

"Galina, that alien blood turned you into a monster that nearly killed your android."

"I what?"

"Don't you remember? You tore that alien in half like it was an egg. Then you came after us. If it wasn't for this one's metal head, he'd be a goner, and probably the rest of us."

Galina forced her neck to turn, made herself look at Celadon. Horrible memories of rage and anger throbbed in the back of her mind.

Celadon tilted his head, showing her the metal plate covering his skull. A large dent in the center had warped the piece.

"I'm so sorry," Galina whispered. "Fuck, I am so sorry."

"Galina." He placed his hand on hers. "It wasn't you that tried to kill me. You were the one who kept it from doing so."

"But that creature was me. I remember what it was feeling, what it wanted to do."

"You stopped when he called your name," Sandoval said. "You didn't listen to the rest of us, but you listened to him."

She recalled being angry and conflicted, remembered having someone in her hands, ready to crush them. Something had stopped her.

"Oh my god. I would have killed you."

"Yes," Celadon said simply.

She just stared, frozen, unable to think or move. She'd almost killed her friend of five years, her closest companion. And she almost hadn't been able to stop herself.

"You're blaming yourself," Celadon continued, watching her. "You're thinking that you can't be trusted, that they should lock you up. That I should stay away from you so I'll be safe."

Galina narrowed her eyes. "Fuck you."

He brushed the insult off and instead grasped her hand. "You made such a terrible decision that it exacted a cost. Part of that cost was a risk to my own life, which I would gladly offer to save the lives of others. The rest, unfortunately, is something you'll bear for the rest of your life. But I will never blame you."

From the doorway, Sandoval sighed loudly. "You may not, but the government might."

"Knowledge of this cannot leave this room," Celadon said.

"Are you serious?" Sandoval asked. "How will you explain that tentacled creature's body?"

"Galina's record as a commander is solid enough to explain her victory."

"And all the biomatter?"

"She injected herself multiple times and shifted in quick succession."

"And everyone who saw it happen?" Galina asked quietly.

"We won't be able to vouch for them, but I will speak to them individually." Celadon looked at Sandoval. "I doubt I will be able to convince you."

"And you'd be right," Sandoval replied. "But you won't have to convince me. If the military finds out about this *chimera*, it will change warfare forever. I have no intention of letting that happen." She threw Galina a half-smile. "Leave the passengers to me. Anything you can say will sound better coming from me."

Celadon paused, then nodded.

"Thank you," Galina said. "Although I feel like I'm going to be living a lie."

"You will be," Sandoval said. "But in the long run, I think it's for the best. The only question is if we'll see the chimera again."

Galina froze.

"That remains to be seen," Celadon said. "But if it does, I will make sure that she doesn't hurt anyone."

"See that you do. I'll go talk to the passengers now." She turned and then paused, an amused smile on her face. "As much as you gripe about him, you might want to hold on to that android. Whatever connection you have, I think it saved your life."

With a wink, Sandoval slipped through the door. Galina felt Celadon's eyes on her again.

Clearing her throat, Galina mumbled, "I, uh, owe you an apology. Several apologies."

"For what?"

"For what I said. I don't want you to leave. You're the only one who can deal with my impulse control."

His lip twitched. "Impulse control isn't your problem."

"Yes, it fucking is, and your head is proof." Grabbing his uniform, Galina pulled him close. "Don't leave me, Celadon. I can't do this without you."

He put his hand over hers, warm and strong. "I'll never leave you."

"You think you can survive being with me?" Galina asked, allowing herself a weak smirk.

Celadon grinned, the first real grin she'd seen since the accident. "I can survive anything you throw at me.

Chimera."

If you liked this story, I've got more coming. Join my newsletter for a free short story, monthly updates, and more!

How much is a life worth?

Zyn doesn't need anyone or anything. Her life is simple: fix things and sell them on the black market. It's not much, but it keeps her alive.

When she finds a living raptor roaming the streets, she can't believe her luck. With a few cybernetic enhancements, it'll fetch a price high enough she can leave her miserable life behind.

But for an ex-R9 soldier, the memories of her past life threatens her plan and forces her to make a choice, one that may not end well for either of them.

Get this short story for free at lenamjohnson.com/newsletter

ACKNOWLEDGMENTS

When I began this story, I knew that something dark and terrible haunted the underbelly of the *Sonora*, and I had to find out what it was. I couldn't have done it without my community and my support.

Thanks to Stephanie for the invaluable feedback, Amy for the encouragement and the opportunity to get this story in front of readers, Sheena for an awesome edit, and Mom for the encouragement.

Thanks to you, dear reader, for giving this story a chance.

ABOUT THE AUTHOR

Lena M. Johnson is a science fiction author from Colorado who is obsessed with dinosaurs and cats. She has been published in various anthologies where she writes about badass women in futuristic worlds. Follow her for news of her upcoming novel, cat pictures, and terrible puns.

Photo by the author

f facebook.com/authorlenamjohnson

instagram.com/Authorlenamjohnson

threads.net/@Authorlenamjohnson

X x.com/lenamjohnson

Made in the USA
Monee, IL
12 October 2024

67079514R00059